My Life in Clothes

Other Works by Summer Brenner

Fiction

I-5, A Novel of Crime, Transport, and Sex
The Missing Lover
Presque nulle part
One Minute Movies
Dancers and the Dance
The Soft Room

Poetry

From the Heart to the Center
Everyone Came Dressed as Water

Fiction for Young People

Richmond Tales, Lost Secrets of the Iron Triangle
Ivy, Tale of a Homeless Girl in San Francisco

My Life in Clothes

STORIES BY

Summer Brenner

 RED HEN PRESS | *Pasadena, CA*

My Life in Clothes
Copyright © 2010 by Summer Brenner
All rights reserved

Versions of these stories first appeared in *Exquisite Corpse, New Blind Date, Processed World, Pangolin Papers, Shuffle Boil,* and *Web del Sol.*

Book layout by Elizabeth Davis
Book design by Mark E. Cull

Brenner, Summer.
  My life in clothes : stories / by Summer Brenner.—1st ed.
    p. cm.
  ISBN 978-1-59709-163-3
  I. Title.
  PS3552.R386M9 2010
  813'.54—dc22

                         2010025155

The Annenberg Foundation, the James Irvine Foundation, the Los Angeles County Arts Commission, and the National Endowment for the Arts partially support Red Hen Press.

First Edition

Published by Red Hen Press
Pasadena, CA
www.redhen.org

Acknowledgments

Special thanks to Ella Baff, Felix Brenner, Laura Chester, Linda Norton, and Jane White who read versions of this work and generously provided me with their thoughtful comments.

for Nancy

Foreword

Despite my mother's efforts to tame me, I resisted, holding onto my creature nature until the day she informed me I would no longer be running naked in the yard or showering with daddy. It took a few scoldings before I was transformed from colt to show-pony: a proper reflection of whichever laundered, starched, pressed, brushed, straightened, zippered, tied, and buttoned garment was placed upon me.

The first dress I adored was pimpled dotted-Swiss, the color of lemonade, worn on the occasion of my fourth birthday. Next was delicious apricot taffeta strewn with flocked leaves. At ten, the treasure in the closet was kitten gray linen accented with a pink velvet collar and sash. Every year, there was an excursion to downtown Atlanta to buy a pair of Capezio party shoes, gracefully-shaped velvet flats with straps that crossed the instep and hooked onto two ivory buttons.

My high school wardrobe was underwritten by summer jobs, and after my first year of college, I was hired to counsel teens leaving home for schools in other climes.

As I got older, income decreased and ingenuity increased. I discovered my calling as a sartorial dowser, gifted at excavating treasures from thrift stores, flea markets, and sidewalk free boxes. After terrible trials and errors, I learned to sew. Riding west across the continent, I embroidered and crocheted. I constructed a skirt of ragged suede scraps which proved too heavy to wear; and an aubergine jerkin covered in cowry shells, part Elizabethan, part Sioux.

Either lost or recycled, almost nothing of these efforts remains except the stories. I shall let them tell you about *My Life in Clothes*.

Contents

When in doubt, wear red.

—Bill Blass

The Dressmaker

In 1903, my grandfather, Moshe Auerbach, walked from Tavrig (Taurage) in Lithuania to Germany. He walked to escape the Czar's army. It was said after twenty years of military service, no one returned from the Czar's army a whole man. He walked with money (sewn into his shirt) which he traded for a ticket (on the *SS Breslau*) to sail to America. He was eighteen years old.

Moshe intended to disembark in Mobile, but because of yellow fever, the port was quarantined. Instead, he returned by ship to Baltimore and followed the trail of his four brothers (Simon, Charlie, Philip, and Ralph) from Maryland to Atlanta. He began as a peddler, traveling by mule-drawn wagon to small country towns and sharecropper farms, selling notions: pots, pans, needles, spools of thread, brushes, and brooms.

"Jew man here!" was the cry throughout the countryside.

Moshe Auerbach, Americanized to Morris Abelman, was determined to become a success. He opened a retail grocery store beside Piedmont Park. He became a wholesaler. During the bonanza years of the 1920s, he established a mill to manufacture chicken feed and flour. The mill thrived, especially in the Great Depression, when few people could afford store-bought bread and returned to home-style baking.

By 1933, after decades of toil, Morris Abelman was a rich man. He wintered in Miami Beach at the Roney Plaza. He summered in the mountains outside Asheville.

On weekdays, he donned a tailor-made silk suit, a starched Egyptian cotton shirt, and a Rep Stripe tie. Every morning he ate his bowl of stewed prunes (his motto: *no grease, no gravy*) and afterwards was chauffeured to his mill in downtown Atlanta, an address so desolate it could have been a hundred miles rather than a short drive from the Abelman mansion in Druid Hills.

Puritan Mills was located beside Buttermilk Bottom, a black section of town (the eponymous name alone indicates what a sour place it was). The houses in Buttermilk Bottom were virtually huts, their windows often covered with cardboard, their roofs with tar paper. The front yards and hilly unpaved roads were red Georgia clay that turned slick and nearly impassible in the rain.

Puritan Mills was a one-storey brick office building and an attached warehouse that abutted Magnum Street, a narrow strip of asphalt that accommodated loading docks as well as parked trucks. At one end of the congestion was a view of Atlanta's burgeoning city skyline, and at the other a sausage factory whose offal smells made us gag.

The entrance to Puritan Mills was hardly suggestive of a fortune. It opened directly into a warren of windowless cubicles. The women who worked in the office were white, but my grandfather had a kitchen constructed in the back of the warehouse where two black women baked all day. They baked and taste-tested biscuits, pies, and bread. They tried out new combos of baking powder, flour, and salt. My grandfather wanted to find and patent the formula for the perfect self-rising biscuit. In the 1950s, a trio of country musicians sang a jingle on TV, a testimony to perfection:

My-T-Pure self-rising flour
My-T-Pure is all y'all need

After Morris had established himself as a merchant, between his station as immigrant peddler and lofty manufacturer, he married

Anna Aron of New York City. Twelve years his junior, she was beautiful, penniless, stylish, and shrewd. On the eve of their engagement, Morris promised her a maid, and from that day forward, my grandmother would live by the credo: *A woman's maid is everything.*

Anna's two insatiable passions were shopping and gambling. She played canasta twice a week and mahjong on Saturday. While traveling, she preferred cruise ships with slot machines and card tables. In Florida, she frequented the horse races at Gulfstream and the greyhound races in West Palm. Whether it was a trip to the Orient or Aegean, what titillated her most were the bingo scores.

When she visited Paris, she wrote a postcard home: *Drove by the Louvre today.* My parents howled, and even as a child, I understood why the observation was so painfully funny.

Anna returned from her travels with trunks of bibelots: alabaster eggs, lace fans, porcelain figurines. Once her own house was filled, she filled her daughters' homes. After Peggy and I were born, she indulged us with foreign dolls (outfitted in their native costumes) and dresses from Italy and France.

Anna also passed along her beauty secrets: stiff egg whites mixed with Witch Hazel for facials; blueberries applied to eyelashes as dye; perfume never sprayed directly on the body but in the air so it could mist over skin and hair. Anna would leave this world a redhead, carrying on the tradition of my great-grandmother, who dropped dead at eighty on the New York subway en route to the beauty parlor.

Most interesting to Peggy and me was the family dressmaker, Mr. Emile, who worked out of a cluttered studio in Garden Hills. It was obvious no one ever swept or tidied up. Threads and shreds of fabric littered his floor. However, underneath the disarray pulsed lively possibilities. Bolts of material, boxes of buttons, boards of piping and braid, waiting to be transformed into his creations.

Mr. Emile was an unusual and dramatic sort of man: the way he spoke, the way he dressed. He and my grandmother liked to nestle together (almost intimately) on a chintz-covered bench and pour through magazines, exclaiming (joyfully or with disgust) over the latest fashions. They conferred about his upcoming projects for her: a black organza sailor dress, a cut-velvet evening suit, a pleated chiffon blouse.

When grandmother had finished her business with Mr. Emile, he kissed us girls on both cheeks, a habit he told us he'd acquired in the finest couture houses of Paris. He kissed Anna on the back of her hand, waving us off with a handkerchief.

Anna said he was her favorite person in the world.

While our grandmother had resources for almost anything, there was no help for my grandfather's aging. It was on a return trip from Europe that Morris first showed signs of wear. At Customs, he failed to declare his Patek Philippe watch (purchased the week before in Geneva). After the watch was confiscated for inspection, he began to cry. He could not be consoled. Although he was assured by officials that the watch would be returned, he wept like a baby.

Then, at Passover, Morris began to tell the story of his great-uncle, a man kidnaped by robbers and released unharmed because of the beauty of his voice. "And you know what the robbers did to him?" he chuckled as he bounced my baby brother on his thighs.

"I know! I know!" I shouted, waving my arms.

"The robbers said if he don't give them all his money, they going to chop up his body and sell it for sausage."

"No, grandpa, that isn't true!" Peggy cried.

"They took out a big butcher knife," Morris continued. "They took the middle finger first. They cut it off."

"No, grandpa!" we protested. We wanted to hear the real story of how he sang so beautifully the bandits let him go.

"They call him Christ killer," Morris hissed. "He begin to sing in pain."

"No, grandpa!"

"They tell him if he don't stop singing, they cut out his tongue."

"Marguerite! Edith!" Anna shrieked. "Your father is losing his mind."

The next week, it was confirmed. Morris was diagnosed with dementia. Arrangements were made for him to leave Atlanta. He went to live in a sanitarium in the center of the state where over a half-century before he had sold buttons and pans.

"I know you," he said to everyone he met.

"Yessir," they replied.

"You my brothers," he insisted.

"Yessir," they reassured him.

"Leave these men alone," my grandmother whispered. "They're *schvartzes.*"

"It don't matter," he said. "They my brothers, too."

When Morris Abelman died, the service filled the city's largest funeral home. A hundred cars followed the family limousine into the cemetery.

A few days after his death, Anna debated who could distract her from the trouble (grief mingled with inconvenience) of losing a husband of forty years.

"I'm going out," she told her maid.

Mr. Emile stood at his studio window, staring at the scuffed shoes trudging by. A monotony broken by a pair of expensive alligator pumps that belonged to Anna Aron Abelman.

"Mr. Emile," she cried with relief, taking her seat on the bench.

Mr. Emile went to his work table. Anna liked listening to the rhythmic clicks of the pinking shears. It recalled the years she rode the subway downtown to work as a secretary. She was sixteen with a wardrobe comprised of two serge dresses (navy and gray), a crepe wool skirt, three blouses (two cotton, one silk), three sweaters, a jacket, two hats, one hat pin, and a threadbare coat.

"I supported my mother and sisters when I was a girl," Anna shrugged. "But who wants to work?"

Mr. Emile looked up from yards of dove-colored gaberdine. "I like to work," he said.

"You do what you want."

"I surround myself with beauty," he smiled.

Anna glanced at the chaotic room. She saw nothing beautiful about it. "When I was a child, I looked into the future of an ugly life."

"You did well," he said.

"My mother, she had nothing. My father was a bum. My daughters, who never washed a stocking in their lives, they don't know what ugly is."

On Saturday, Peggy and I were dropped at our grandmother's to keep her company. She was dressed in black which we understood was the color of death and mourning (we were still too young to wear black).

"There's no ice cream," we complained. In summer, Anna always made us foamy ginger-ale floats. In winter, she served warm coffee-milk with sugar.

We set out from her elegant apartment on Peachtree Street, down Ponce de Leon Avenue to the Piggly Wiggly. We passed bars and decrepit resident hotels. Friendly drunks stumbled by. Old people and cripples asked us for money. Except for Buttermilk Bottom, I had never seen where poor people lived. I never knew poor people were sometimes white.

"It's ugly here," Peggy said.

On steamy nights in Harlem, Anna's mother led them to the roof of the tenement house where there was usually a breeze from the river. They slept on the roof, and all night the smell of tar wove through the girl's dreams. In the morning, her face and hands were streaked with soot.

"You don't know ugly!" Anna burst out.

"Grandma?" We wondered how we had offended her.

She folded her arms around our shoulders. "What I come from, what grandpa came from," she said, "it's in another world."

Accessories to Crime

Soon after my tenth birthday, my mother, Marguerite, took me on a tour of Europe. Not the grand tour of debutantes but a two-week jaunt in the company of a dozen exemplary citizens from Atlanta: middle-aged, church-going professionals, bankers, dentists, lawyers, accountants, and their wives.

My mother stood out among the matrons. She was younger and slimmer as well as beautiful with sophisticated taste and a short, chic haircut. For evening strolls through the capitals, she wore a charcoal gray wool suit with a voluptuous gray fox collar. For bus rides and days tramping through museums and palaces, she put on camelhair slacks and a matching cashmere sweater. In whatever attire wherever we went, she drew the attentive gaze from men of every nationality.

For Marguerite, it was Harrods that confirmed we had arrived in Europe. "At last, we can go to Harrods!" she exclaimed with an ardor reserved exclusively for clothes.

Harrods sounded so muffled to my ear. Had the L accidentally been omitted?

"Harolds?" I timidly asked.

"Har-RODS," mother snapped. "The finest store in the entire world."

Before the Tower and after St. Paul, between lunch at The Savoy and tea in Piccadilly, mother hailed a black cab, as big as a sarcophagus, to carry us from the Strand to Brompton Road. I stood on the sidewalk in awe, staring at Harrods' flags, crests, and crenelations. My mother was positively correct. Harrods was the finest store in the entire world.

In May, few winter coats remained on the racks. In my size, there was only one, fabricated from heavy, coarse, Scottish wool, faintly purple like boiled rhubarb, and thoroughly unbecoming. Its single redeeming feature was a half-dozen carved wooden buttons that I immediately began to twirl.

"Stop fidgeting!" mother commanded. "If you don't ruin it, next winter you'll be glad to have a coat from Harrods."

From London, our tour flew to Brussels where we were met by a bus, a driver, and a guide. Oskar was historian, polyglot, and hedonist, who promised to introduce the Georgian provincials to European wines and risqué art. Although a child, I would soon be privy to both.

The itinerary transported us by bus across Belgium, along the Rhine, and into Switzerland. Wherever we stopped, I acquired a postcard or cloisonné charm to remember the quaint towns, the castles and churches, the rivers and farms, and the cuisine so different from my own.

Late spring outside Bern was an inspired combination of wild flowers and snow-capped peaks. Our hotel was a chalet, decorated with wide shutters and painted barge board. I pranced across its lawn and passed two Alpine days with my middle-age companions, clambering around mountainsides and eating fondue.

On the morning of our departure, I overheard my mother cursing in the bathroom.

"I can't get the goddamn thing off," she cried.

I peeked through the door. Armed with tweezers and hairbrush, Marguerite hovered in a contorted position over a brass and porcelain faucet handle attached to the bathroom sink. As soon as she spied me, she threw the hairbrush at the floor in a pique and tried prying the handle loose with her hands.

"Why?" I asked in alarm.

She wrestled on. "I can't get it off."

Like most children, I was thoroughly cognizant of the minute shades of difference between taking, borrowing, lending, and stealing. In defense of my mother, I rationalized. Perhaps, she had asked permission. Perhaps, the antique (and likely worthless) fixtures would not be missed. Perhaps, my mother knew that the proprietor intended to replace the "old things" with modern, dependable ones and had enlisted my mother's help.

Marguerite wiped her forehead, dripping with effort. She had broken a fingernail, and her elbow was bloody from pressing down on the chipped drain. "Get over here and help."

I hung back.

"Hold on while I tug."

I slouched to the sink. Outside was my escape into a valley of flowers. However, I lacked the requisite courage to jump onto the cobblestone courtyard and run away.

"I'll wait downstairs," I attempted, but the words stuck in my throat.

She steadied my hand and pushed it forward as a vice. Finally, she succeeded in loosening a rusted screw. "That's quite a lot of work," she sighed, balancing the object on her palm. "But it's beautiful, isn't it?"

I puzzled over the question. My appreciation of beauty did not include bathroom fixtures.

"What are you staring at?" My mother's voice shrilled with its familiar accusation that I was always staring off at something.

"Mountains," I mumbled.

Mother gave the scenery a dismissive glance. "I shall paint our shutters blue, too," she announced in reference to the old-fashioned stone and brick house she and my father had recently bought. Its architecture, in fact, was identical to a chalet with shuttered casement windows, a slate roof, beamed ceilings, and a stairway encased in a circular tower. "That exact blue," she pointed to a wing of the genuine Swiss chalet that extended along the winding drive.

By now, she had the other handle. "These," she said, holding up the spoils, "will go in the powder room." Indeed, the powder room was the most extravagant corner of the house, decorated with a silver leaf dressing table and oval mirror swagged with crystal ropes.

She stuffed the two handles into her purse. It was time to leave. Closets and chest of drawers had been emptied and suitcases repacked, including the coat from Harrods.

"You haven't forgotten anything, have you?" mother asked.

"No," I faltered. On the contrary, if only I could retrieve the whatchamacallits and screw them back in place.

"Why are you standing around?" Mother poked me with an umbrella. "Pick up the bags and get downstairs."

Underneath the bus, the luggage hatch was propped open. Everyone had settled into their seats, some preferring the front next to Oskar, others stretched out in back to snooze.

"Good morning, madame, mademoiselle," Oskar greeted us cheerily.

We nodded and took our customary seats midway down the aisle.

"Ready?" he asked, counting the passengers again.

The bus door slammed shut. The engine turned over. Several nauseating wafts of diesel smoke drifted through the open windows as the behemoth rolled backwards into the parking lot. The driver then coasted towards the gravel road that wound across a bright, spring green valley and down to the highway.

"Stop!" A ruddy-faced man yelled from the hotel verandah. "Stop the bus!"

Through the windshield, everyone watched an oversized figure leap down the chalet stairs, waving his arms like the blades of a windmill.

The driver pressed the brakes. The concierge dashed up the steps of the bus, through the door, and gasping for breath, bellowed, "There is missing."

While he and Oskar consulted in German, the genteel tourists from Georgia tried to decipher what he meant. "Missing?" Bewildered looks raced from front to back.

Oskar shuddered. It was very unpleasant news. "The bathroom hardware in one of our rooms has been removed," he grumbled.

An explanation that only increased everyone's confusion. "Bathroom what? Removed from where?"

A humiliated Oskar said, "We cannot leave until they're returned."

Still puffing, the concierge concurred.

An oceanic murmur rose. "More than one?" No one could imagine.

I shut my eyes, wishing to be whisked away, transported to a mountaintop where I might spend my remaining days with Heidi, Grandfather, and the goats. Anywhere but on this bus.

When my eyes reopened, Oskar and the concierge had not budged. They stood solidly in place, eyeing each passenger in turn.

"The room number is 217," they finally said.

"Wasn't that you, Marguerite?" one of the bank presidents asked.

"I didn't notice," she shrugged.

"I was in 215," someone asserted.

Coolly, Marguerite felt inside her pockets. Coolly, she checked under the seat. Then, pausing as an afterthought, she opened her purse and groped inside.

"You mean these?" She yanked out two antique brass and porcelain handles, engraved with *chaud* and *froid*.

The concierge nodded icily as they were passed to the front of the bus. Two dozen censoring eyes fell upon us.

Mother rose. She laid a hand on my hunched shoulder.

I recoiled, clasping and unclasping my fingers, bowing my head in a futile prayer.

"Sue, can you tell us why you took them?" Her voice quivered but within seconds, it was strong and certain. "Can you tell us why?"

The bus idled as if it were waiting for the answer, too.

My numbness was deeper than an Alpine crevasse, but like an understudy called to her first leading role, I said firmly, "I don't know why."

"Sue doesn't know," Marguerite repeated in case anyone had failed to hear.

Then, rising slowly, I dragged myself to the back of the bus as the engine shifted into gear.

My Life in Clothes

Early on, my cousin, Peggy, discovered that her greatest talent was the ability to turn a boy's simplest request into the world's biggest marvel. "Peggy, can I walk you home?" they begged. "Peggy, can I sit beside you at the picture show?" In response, Peggy's chin would tilt, her gaze lift, her lips moisten, her calves flex, and her breasts rise. Peggy was irresistible.

By the end of high school, after she had been squeezed, groped, rubbed, pounded, and humped, she eloped (out of sheer exhaustion) with the next young man who asked. (It was her third proposal of the summer.)

Fifteen years later, she returned to Atlanta, a divorced mother of two. Buckhead was no longer a small suburban center. It was its own center, bursting with commerce and style. The owner of a popular bar (that prided itself on imported beers) was a local boy, glad to hire Peggy. The patrons of the Acme were glad, too. They were from the old crowd.

Peggy recognized their names and faces, but what they recognized in her was sacred. They had never given her up. They were still seeking a way to leave their mark on Peggy, for above everything else, she represented the moment when they believed they would leave their mark on the world.

"I never saw a girl who attracted so many boys," her mother reminisced nearly everyday. "Remember whosit who tried to climb down the chimney? And the night Charlie Key drove over the lawn? There were so many corsages in the fridge, we couldn't find room for leftovers." Edith's voice choked with admiration. She had conceived a blond, willowy wildcard in a gene pool that normally favored short, heavy, and mousy brown.

"Men don't court women anymore," Peggy informed her mother. "If a man has money, he doesn't spend it on a woman. He expects her to have her own money and spend it on herself."

"The night Wash Smith invited a string quartet to play under your window? And Cyrus Temple, etching your initials on his arm with hydrochloric acid?"

"They weren't my initials," Peggy protested.

"His mother said you ought to be banished from the state before you wrecked another boy's sanity. It was wonderful," Edith sighed nostalgically.

"It isn't fashionable now to be romantic."

"Pooh!" her mother said. "Men are as primitive as they have always been."

"I saw Charlie last night," Peggy reported. It made her feel fifteen to say his name.

"He ruined my camellias. He ran that blue Impala around my yard like a monkey on a trike."

"He's looks the same."

"Don't be vague, Peggy. Is he available?"

"There were grease stains on his tie."

"You weren't so critical then."

"He pals around with Wash."

"I suppose he made something of himself."

"He's a drunk."

Edith shook her head despairingly. Peggy had had every opportunity, natural and otherwise, to make a good catch. It wasn't too late. "You ought to do something productive with your looks while they last. Damnit, Peggy, you rode the senior float and now you're a barmaid."

"Waitress," she corrected.

"I thought the job would take your mind off your troubles, but it's making you bitter. And you're irritating your wrinkles when you smile. Tell me more about Wash."

"He wrote a screenplay. He says it's going to be a movie."

Cocking her head like an ingénue, Edith asked, "Is he going to put you on the silver screen?"

"It's about four gay men who die of AIDS."

"Wash is a fairy?" Edith's celebrity future melted into a blur.

Peggy's past was springing up with ardor. Charlie Key sent her a dozen roses wrapped in an expensive silk scarf. Over the weekend, Zip Feinstein stopped in town for his father's birthday and offered to give her money (lots of money) for a new car. Wash invited her to visit him in Hollywood (the film was going forward). And Jim Gerber telephoned from Santa Fe, wanting to know what happened to the school's best-looking girl. He offered to fly her out. "To get a look," he said.

"Guess who came up to me in the store today?" Edith tittered. "Cy Temple introduced himself in the produce department. He even showed me the scar from the acid."

"He showed you?"

"Pooh! It's nothing. He apologized up and down for the trouble he caused back then. He is the nicest man. He is just your type. He loves to travel. He loves kids. He's got a steady job."

When Cy walked into the Acme, Peggy didn't recognize him. He sat in her section and ordered a Corona.

"Remember me, Cyrus Temple, the weirdo?" He giggled and lifted his glass in a toast. "I saw your mother, did she tell you?"

"She told me," Peggy said.

"I bet it happens all the time. Boys stopping by, swearing that you're the prettiest girl in the world. You haven't changed."

"I've changed," she said wearily.

"Remember your fuzzy white sweater?"

"Angora blend," Peggy mused.

"The round-collared blouse with little flowers?"

"Liberty of London."

"And tasseled?"

"Bass Weegens," she interrupted. She remembered every article of clothing from high school. Some of it, she had kept.

Cy pushed up his sleeve. "And this?"

Peggy looked at the lump of scar tissue. She was surprised. It did resemble her initials.

Cyrus Temple drank five beers. He stayed until closing, lingering outside the bar, hoping to drive her home.

"The prettiest girl with the biggest freak, who would believe you're talking to me?" He pinched himself.

"That nonsense doesn't matter now," Peggy said.

"We never had a chance to talk. I mean, really talk."

"Nobody did. We were going through the motions. Like clothes, trying things on, taking things off."

"I adored you," Cy whimpered. "That's a fact."

Peggy turned away. She didn't want to hear it. She had heard enough.

Mustering his courage, Cy swivelled Peggy around and smacked his lips against hers. When his tongue darted into her mouth, she clamped down her teeth as hard as she could.

"Aieeeee!" he shrieked.

Peggy had already started to run. Into the darkness, past the shops and restaurants of Buckhead, she ran like a panther, the most desired animal in the world.

The Wallet

I should have been home asleep with the baby, but in the late afternoon, my supervisor called to ask if I could help with a presentation. After dinner, I put the baby down at her house, and since the work took longer than expected, I didn't leave until midnight.

The main street of town was deserted. I drove along slowly, dreamily until a phantom rose out of the sidewalk. It was Peter (my husband), walking slowly and dreamily too, with both his arms draped around a strange girl. At that instant, my love for him drained away. Later, I wished (with all my heart) I had run the car over the curb into his body. But instead, I went home and threw up.

The next morning, I discredited what I saw. I called Marco where Peter sometimes spent the night so they could rehearse without disturbing the baby.

"Marco?" I asked calmly. "Could I have possibly seen Peter in town late last night? With his tennis partner?"

"Lisa McElduff?" Marco sounded calm, too.

"Maybe it was Lisa McElduff. I don't really know Lisa."

"Hasn't Peter told you about Lisa?"

I hung up. For a few minutes, I waited for a plan of revenge to formulate. The plan was trite (since *The Count of Monte Cristo*, there's never been anything original about revenge). I vowed to leave Peter and never let him see our baby again.

I attacked every drawer and closet, piling up in Peter's studio whatever I had made or given him: lovingly hand-sewn shirts, beautiful crocheted mufflers, an embroidered denim jacket, darned socks, many books of poetry, sable brushes, a bagpipe, and two pairs of silk boxers. All of these, I methodically (and gleefully) tore, shredded, crumpled, and cracked. Then, I dumped a can of red paint over the lot.

Next, I burned his letters to me. And tossed out a box of memorabilia, the items that had initiated me into womanhood: my first bra (28 AAA), my first garter belt, the empty but still stinky first pack of cigarettes (Winston box), a stained Kotex belt, the blouse I had on when I French kissed Steve Fink, a straw pillbox hat pinned with dried rosebuds that I wore when I married Peter, and a green plastic wallet from sixth grade containing my Buckhead library card, a lucky silver dollar, and a picture of me taken in a photobooth at Myrtle Beach.

I traveled light to California. Suitcase, diaper bag, baby.

"Peter called," my cousin announced at the airport. "He asked if I knew where you were."

"And?"

"I told him you were on a plane."

"And?"

"He started to cry. He said you destroyed his life and his studio. He wondered if I knew why."

"Because it felt good," I said without guile. Harsh as it was, it registered as less severe than what Peggy did when she left Freddie Mason. After she found Freddie in bed at home with his lab assistant, she cut the left arm off all his sweaters, jackets, shirts, and coats and snipped the ends of his ties.

In California, I cried, too, for weeks, the baby and I both. Sometimes, Peggy joined us. Once we got started, there was no end of inspiration and regret. And the baby just couldn't help herself.

Peggy helped me find a cottage in the Berkeley hills. We took walks to the park. We relaxed in cafés. It was a serene, uncomplicated time.

Peter often called. He wanted to know how I had transmogrified into a vengeful person. I told him people were capable of anything. He only had to read the newspaper (once in a while) to know that. When he said he was coming to California, I tried not to react. I tried to be what the Buddhists call *detached*.

"Don't you want me to come?" he asked.

"I don't need you to come," I told him, thinking of the past tranquil months with the baby. "What about McElduff?"

Peter called me a fool. A week later, he arrived with whatever belongings I hadn't ruined. Stuff enough to shatter the peace inside my tiny space. He was happy to see us, and as it turned out, we were happy to see him, too.

Years have passed since that period of separation and reunion. Peter and I have fought, reconciled, and fought again. Through our child, time has assumed a forward propulsion. She has gotten bigger, stronger, louder. While the changes in our lives appear minute, hers have been colossal.

We have stayed in Berkeley. We now live in a bigger cottage in a less attractive area. Peter works as a handyman. I'm a receptionist at a gym. Rents have escalated, and we aren't sure we can afford to stay much longer. Although crime rates have fallen, fear has risen. Parents are urged to have their children finger-printed (in case of kidnaping). The faces of missing youngsters appear on milk cartons, staring at us every morning over breakfast. Our neighbors spend substantial sums on alarms, window bars, and guard dogs. Everyone has grown paranoid.

When a small box arrived from an unknown sender, I observed it cautiously. It was poorly taped, and my full name, large and tentative, was written as if someone didn't know how to spell. It was post-marked Atlanta, but the return address was Owen Huff in Roswell, Georgia.

I put the box outside on the porch until Peter came home.

"Do you know anyone in Roswell?" he asked.

When I was growing up, Roswell was a distant outpost, synonymous with banishment itself.

"Huff doesn't ring a bell?"

"Maybe, my cousin sent a bomb."

"Impossible," Peter said. My cousin, Malcolm, had recently initiated a nasty lawsuit with his sister, Peggy, over their inheritance.

Peter picked up the rectangular box, the size of a pair of children's shoes. He gently shook it. "Do you want me to call the police?"

"No," I said.

"Then we'd better open it."

When Sarah ran across the yard, I ordered her to stand back on the sidewalk. "It might be dangerous up here," I advised.

She plunked down on the curb, squirming with excitement while Peter took out a Swiss Army knife and cut the tape. He shook the box again. Gingerly, he pried open two top flaps. Underneath a sheet of the *Dunwoody Crier* were several folded layers of bubble-wrap which made it impossible to see anything.

"Can't I come now?" Sarah shouted.

"We don't know what's in the box."

"Owen Huff is a careful wrapper," Peter said.

As he started to unfold the bubble-wrap, I saw something bright green trapped in the center like a tree frog in an ice floe.

"My wallet!" I cried.

"Did you lose it?" Peter asked.

"My wallet, my wallet!" I waved for Sarah to come up. "This is the wallet I had when I was your age."

Sarah was disinterested.

"Here's my Buckhead library card."

Sarah was indifferent.

"Here's a picture of me at Myrtle Beach. Aren't I hideous?"

Sarah glanced over.

I clutched the wallet to my chest. A missing piece of childhood had returned like a message in a bottle.

"Here's my lucky silver dollar," I said, unzipping the coin purse. "You take it."

Sarah stuck out her hand. A dollar, even silver, was also uninteresting.

Buried deeper than the wallet was an envelope with my name. Inside Owen Huff reported that his father, Owen Huff senior, had recently died.

Peter read aloud:

About a dozen years back when I was in school, I went on a field trip.

I do not remember exactly where I was exactly but I found this wallet and intending to return it but being I did not know how. I'd forgotten until daddy passed away. We moved around a lot but liked to save special things and took them with us. I was cleaning out his attic and found the cute wallet in a box with the cute picture and lucky $, you better needed it. I called your last name in the phone book and they given me your address in California.

Sincerely, Owen Huff

"That's a strange thing," Peter pondered. "Do you remember losing your wallet when you were a child?"

"No, I kept it for years," I admitted. "I kept it in a box. Then, something came over me one day, and I threw it away."

Belgian Lace

Although Marguerite never worked a day in her life, she experienced the frustrations and tedium of the humdrum, workaday world. In furies and fits, she attacked gas pumps and doors. She barked at traffic signals. She raced around Atlanta, cursing her dead husband who, unlike her own father, never made enough money to hire a chauffeur.

Signal lights, however, were trivial compared to the maledictions directed at telephone operators, doctors, insurance adjusters, manicurists, repair men, stock brokers, and clerks. In the couture department at Rich's, she was known as "code blue" (meaning anyone would rather die than have to wait on Marguerite Breen).

"If people could just do what they're supposed to," that was her lament. And her job, so to speak, was to let everyone know when they weren't properly doing theirs.

This week's grievance? The price tag on a brassiere at Neiman Marcus. "Two-hundred-and-twenty-five dollars?" Her eyebrows arched dangerously. "It's an outrage what they think they can get away with."

"They're imported from Paris in France," the salesgirl explained.

"I know where Paris is," Marguerite seethed. "I want to speak to the buyer."

"She's out to lunch, ma'am."

"Then, who's supposed to be in charge?"

The girl disappeared behind a curtain and reappeared with a heavy-set man. "Mrs. Breen," he greeted her affably.

"Who do you think you are? Charging $225 for a flimsy nothing?" The launch was loud enough to be heard in Shoes.

"We don't regulate prices here," he flushed.

"Then, I'd like you to telephone Dallas," she said, fondling the satin bow tucked between two perfect baby-blue cups. In all her experience, first-class and worldwide, she had never seen such workmanship.

"It is the correct price, madam." His head lifted with loyalty and pride. "See the code?"

"I see nothing but a ridiculous price tag."

"French design, Belgian lace," his closing argument.

"Who the hell is going to pay that?" Sportswear heard the shriek. Marguerite pounded the carpet and stomped through the wall of double glass doors. "Who?" She interrogated the parking attendant whose English wasn't qualified to understand the question.

—

Dr. Cohen motioned his patient to the tobacco leather couch. "What has happened to get you so upset?"

Marguerite buried her face in her hands. Her shoulders shook, and her stomach rumbled with chicken salad.

Nearby, Dr. Cohen sat in the wing-chair, swinging a silver fountain pen across his knee. It usually required thirty swings for a patient to compose herself. Marguerite Breen required more. Last year, he suggested she "repress" her feelings.

"Whoever heard of a psychiatrist telling a patient to repress? Especially feelings?" my mother asked me.

A week later, when she returned to the couch, she demanded, "Do you mean I should keep the things that tear me to pieces to myself? And not let other people know what they do to me?"

Even with a medical degree from the Ivy League, the doctor could be intimidated by Marguerite. "Life might be calmer if you did." He said, blending sympathy with caution.

"Calm is not why I was born," she rebutted. "I am a woman of passions, Richard." She was not about to address anyone with less than half her life experience as doctor of anything.

"You spend much of your time getting upset," he reminded her.

"It isn't me who's upset. They're upset because they fail to do anything right. It rubs off on me, that's the problem." Marguerite rose abruptly, brushed off her crushed silk pants, and collapsed back on the pile of cushions. "I had an awful thing happen today."

"Do you want to talk about it?"

"I got the letter Wednesday," she announced. "I got the phone call this morning."

"And?"

"Sue has not visited me in a year. Now, she informs me she'll be coming from California for her cousin's wedding. She'll condescend to stop in Atlanta on the way." Marguerite sputtered. "Sue has never cared about me. She has lived as far away as possible from me. I make the sacrifice and traipse out there, a place I hate, but she is my daughter. That's why I make the effort."

Marguerite gulped a glass of water and handed it to Dr. Cohen for a refill.

"She takes up with shiftless men whom she prefers to me. She has their children who do not know me, who do not call me Nana, who have no idea what I did for Sue when she was growing up."

On two hands, Marguerite inventoried piano and ballet lessons, Girl Scouts, swimming instruction, horseback riding, summer camps, and private schools.

"Of course, I told her the truth, I can't help that. I asked her, 'Who in the hell wants to watch a 45-year-old woman get married?' Then, I reminded her she can't afford to fly across the country. She has to work, doesn't she? She has to support those hungry kids. She doesn't have that kind of money. I'm sure not giving it to her. Get one of her boyfriends to give it to her. I do not have it. I can't buy a new car. I can't take a trip this year. And today, in Neiman-Marcus I sacrificed something I wanted very badly."

Marguerite stopped to catch her breath.

"Invited or not, I won't be going to the wedding. ABC gum is what I told her. Already-Been-Chewed is not what normal people call 'romantic.' A middle-aged woman with dyed hair marrying an orthodontist with a pot belly? If that is romantic, I will shoot myself."

"Perhaps Sue is trying to tell you something about her own choices," Dr. Cohen offered.

"She should have thought of that when she still had her looks," Marguerite said, twisting the skin around her fingers. "My sister struts around Atlanta like the Queen Mother. She set up a registry at Saks. Who in the hell is going to buy china and silver for a woman who has already been married? Twice!"

The doctor stood. That was his signal. Their hour together was up.

Marguerite did not like leaving Dr. Cohen. She disliked the thought of going home. Her apartment was lonely. She could think of no one to call. She had abandoned her old friends, and her new young ones weren't so interesting after all.

"What is it?" she asked him.

"What is what?"

"I've forgotten, damnit."

Forgetfulness was rare. Age had not dimmed Marguerite's accounting abilities. In reverse of nature, anger and frustration had only served to sharpen her wits.

"When you remember, write it down," he suggested.

"Until next week," she said, her face deflating, the fight drained from her body.

Richard Cohen turned to his desk. Beyond the reception area, he could hear the echo of what his patient had failed to say.

"I detest this family!" she screamed. The words ricocheted in the hall as the elevator doors closed behind her.

Lucky Pleats

After several days of record-breaking heat, the temperature finally started to drop. I walked past the blocks of parched gardens to the steamy parking lot behind the grocery store. I mopped my brow, smoothed my cotton pedal pushers, moistened my lips, and sat down on a bench at the back of the store. I tried to quiet my excitement with breathing exercises I once learned for childbirth. They were useless then, useless now.

The situation, however, was comically familiar. Saturday afternoon in a public place, in a parking lot in fact, waiting for Roy as I used to wait years ago when we met in dozens of parking lots behind restaurants, bars, shops, any crowded place out of the way.

I was early, but according to habit, he was precisely on time. You could set a clock by Roy. I slipped into the car (late-model Japanese sedan). There was no temptation to slide across the seat and turn up the radio. In fact, the radio was off, and unlike his vintage Mustang convertible, the car was ordinary.

At a glance, he looked healthy and freshly showered. His eyes sparkled. The tightness in his jaw had relaxed. He wore his standard attire: tight t-shirt emblazoned with a sports logo and faded 501 jeans. The t-shirt accentuated his biceps, and I could recall them wildly pumping whenever he dashed off a set of fingertip push-ups.

As for me, despite the youthful apparel, I looked older.

I first met Roy at the local pool. Initially, there was lunch after laps, and after a few months an invitation to visit him at his studio. I brought along sandwiches and India Pale Ale, and we flopped on the floor (rather than his daybed) to watch the World Series. Halfway through the sixth inning, our restraint reached its limit. I removed my cute cowboy shirt and threw it across the room. In another minute, he threw me onto the narrow bed. And my wonderful, agonizing affair with a married man officially began.

It was Roy who first took me to the track, taught me to read the form, fronted my first bets, and showed me how to translate subtleties into temperament. I learned to sort out the winning attributes: excited but not excitable, proud but not haughty, eager but not nervous, responsive but not servile. In the cheap races, I could spot a good horse going downhill. In the high stakes, I had a sharp eye for newcomers. And like everybody, I sometimes disregarded the form and bet on whim, proving that chance (unless you had an insider tip) was as powerful as reason.

Whenever Roy and I had an opportunity to travel, we favored places with tracks. After a winning day at Gulfstream, we checked into The Biltmore (Coral Gables), a baroque hotel built in the 1920s. That night was the only occasion I ever saw him wear anything remotely formal: a wrinkled manilla linen jacket over a wrinkled white shirt. The jacket fit poorly, but it didn't matter. Roy possessed an air of confidence that always made him look as if he were in the right place at the right time.

As for me, I wore the same lucky dress that I always wore to the races. A navy nylon shirtwaist with flocked polka-dots, accordion-pleated skirt, and rhinestone barrel-shaped buttons. I unearthed it in an Oakland thrift store. Pure vintage '50s like Roy. Every chapter of our romance mimicked the love songs we listened to as kids. Roy was the high school quarterback, and I was the queen on the float.

After a few blocks, I commented, "Like old times."

He didn't understand.

"Parking lots?"

He didn't recall.

"Because you didn't want your wife to see my car at your studio," I chided.

Roy snickered. He and his wife were now divorced.

"Remember the hundred dollar bill I lost at the track?"

He didn't recall that either.

It had dropped out of my pocket, but I found it wedged in a crack of asphalt and nailed the trifecta in the fifth race. The intoxication of winning was as doomed as my love for Roy. Gambler's doom, believing it would last.

"Where should we go?" he asked me.

Since it was cooling down, I suggested a walk at the estuary. We moved slowly because of his bad knee. He talked about himself: celebrities who came to his concerts, the article in *Rolling Stone*, his cameo role in a stylish film.

I waffled between envy and boredom, but in the end, I forgave him. The boasting made him seem more vulnerable than vain.

After rolling through the credits of his career, he turned to the topic of his last girlfriend (from Catalonia). They had separated, too. Boasting again, he mentioned what a commotion her animal appeal had created in his neighborhood. His remarks made me sad. Rather than old, I felt replaced. Our own little legend had drifted out of Roy's mind.

Finally, he checked on the status of my children, my job, my career. Then, he quizzed me about the races.

"I hardly go anymore. When I do, I bet on long-shots. I usually lose." I laughed freely because we had always laughed a lot.

He pried into my private affairs.

"There's nothing to tell."

"You?" he exclaimed, meaning I had been so good at loving him.

"I'm no longer a romantic," I declared as proof of cure.

Instead of wise, I could tell he thought I sounded defeated. He felt sorry for me while I felt liberated. I wanted to claim I was happy, but it was obvious he wouldn't believe me. Since we split up, he thought I had become unlucky.

After a drink, Roy returned me to the parking lot behind the grocery store. He politely took my hand. We gazed at each other, and suddenly, he dove into my neck. A shock, like guzzled whiskey, fired through me.

"Life and the track," he began.

I brushed his cheek with a kiss and opened the car door. As for life and the track, I knew all about it. At the races, everyone was trying to outwit fortune. It was a marvelous and futile spectacle.

I stood for a moment, smiling through the open window. Roy studied me with an adoring look. He turned the key in the ignition and with an urgency, as if these words were to be our last, he cried out, "Don't give up."

The Finished Hem

The last year Roy and I were together, I performed a small miracle on behalf of my neighbor, Mary Chin:

> To whom it may concern:
>
> Mrs. Chin was overcharged for unnecessary work performed at your local garage. I have personally had these charges verified by my own mechanic. She was taken advantage of because of her difficulty with English. I will seek legal counseling on her behalf if you do not reimburse the unnecessary charges.
>
> Thank you.

A month later, Mary and I received letters of apology from corporate headquarters, assuring us a check was on its way. With that news, Mary told me, "You are my best American friend."

In Beijing, Mary had been an accountant, her husband a math teacher. In Berkeley, he washed dishes in a restaurant. She sewed piece-work at an outdoor equipment company.

Before Mary arrived from China, her elderly parents occupied the same small apartment on the third storey of our apartment house. Shabby but efficient, the balconies were crammed with plants, hibachis, and bicycles. Every evening, smells drifted up from the kitchens of the foreign families who lived below.

Mary's father, a minister at a Chinese Christian church, left the People's Republic when she was a baby, fled to Taiwan, and eventually immigrated to California. When Mary arrived in Berkeley, she had not seen her father in forty years.

In September, when Mary was reimbursed for overcharges, Sarah asked me to make her a new skirt for third grade. We went to the fabric store, and I wrote a final note to Roy:

Dear Roy
Stop calling
Stop stopping by
STOP

After a dozen melodramatic break-ups and heady reunions, I was convinced I was happier without him. The empirical proof was fewer backaches and a sweeter temper.

A month later, he wrote back:

PLEASE COME to Slim's
October 28, 9 PM, guest list
I love you. Period. Roy

His new song was the reason for the urgent invitation. It was about us, dedicated to me, and the most forlorn tune ever written. After I told him I would come, I spent two days trying on outfits in a fever of ambivalent feelings. Finally, I settled on a vintage circle skirt, a woven turquoise top, short flat boots, and a pound of silver bracelets.

Following the show, there was another note with a plane ticket to Florida where he was scheduled to start an East Coast tour. He said the song belonged to both of us. Period.

I rearranged Sarah's carpool schedule. I lied at work. I packed a suitcase of beach clothes with the pieces of Sarah's gingham skirt (material she'd picked out with a pattern that included a peplum waist) and flew to Miami.

Roy picked me up in a limo strewn with flowers and a portable bar stocked with Dixie cups and champagne. By the time he put me back on the plane, I had basted Sarah's skirt.

He had two more weeks of concerts and a Thanksgiving in-law visit in Boston planned with his wife. I fumed all the way back to California and wrote a farewell note over the Sierra Nevada.

Roy didn't respond. He was busy. The song was a hit.

My withdrawal symptoms were the same: acute backache followed by sadness, a few weeks of resignation, and finally relief.

Meanwhile, Sarah's skirt sat on a shelf, reminding me of the beautiful drive with Roy across the Florida Keys.

Six months later, I picked up the phone. "Roy?"

"Miss Sue?"

That instant, we began retracing the familiar blueprint. By Sunday, all signs had returned. I was immobilized on the sofa with an ice pack and a bottle of Motrin, cursing my lack of resolve.

Then, I spied Sarah's unhemmed skirt. Third grade was almost over, but it was still big enough to fit her. I grabbed the skirt and hobbled to Mary's apartment.

"My best friend," Mary enunciated. Her English had improved.

She inserted thread into her industrial machine, adjusted the bobbin, and depressed a foot pedal the size of a cookie sheet. The needle raced over the hemline. A minute later, Mary smiled with satisfaction, folded the skirt, and handed it back to me.

At last, I thought, it's finished.

Skin Deep

My neighbor, Saraswati, was born in Mauritius. Her mother called her *poulet noir* ("black chicken") because she was darker than her siblings. She treated her daughter like a servant. Saraswati left home at a young age, traveled to India, and joined an ashram where she met and married an American. I was told they were Hari Krishnas although I never heard her chanting or saw religious markings on her face.

Saraswati was an extremely friendly woman in contrast to her husband. "My husband is an excellent man," she frequently told me, shaking her dark, pretty head. "His studies require him to go away."

Saraswati operated a day-care center in a two-storey, brown shingled house. Weekdays, weekends, days, nights, she was busy with other people's children and her own. Despite the traffic, the house and yard were immaculate. In the late afternoon, she could be found sweeping the street with a short, handleless broom, reporting the latest neighborhood gossip.

"This morning a couple stopped by the fence at a devilishly early hour to admire my roses," she confided to me.

The tall, tangerine rose trees that lined her front yard were perfect. No black spot or rust. As she spoke, I conjured dawn meanderings with a lover.

"They had a basket and shears," she shrilled, changing gears and thrusting her small head into my face. "I yelled at them from the window, 'You get the fuck away from my roses.' Then, I called the police."

Saraswati was always calling the police. Last spring, after a terrorist was arrested, local news crews appeared seeking photos of the cottage where the culprit once lived. Several handmade NO TRESPASSING signs were posted on her fences, gates, and doors. She told me a TV anchorman threatened her when she refused to let him enter her yard.

"He made a disgusting gesture at my crotch. He shouted that he wanted to fuck me in the ass." She repeated "in the ass" several times as her tiny, slack-jawed daughters clung to their mother's skirt.

When she finally lowered her voice, it was to point out a black youth with an Afro who had recently moved in next door. "He's dealing drugs from the car," she said.

I glanced at the sedate Honda parked in front of Saraswati's house. She had already called the police.

The next time I saw her, I simply waved. I was too tired to walk over and listen. I could no longer sort out vigilance from paranoia. However, a wave sufficed for friendship. That evening, Saraswati telephoned to ask if I would drive her to the hospital when she went into labor. Her excellent husband had already been away many months and was not scheduled to return until after their baby's due date.

A week later, she called again with news that labor had started. Half-asleep, I prepared to drive to the hospital and hold Saraswati's hand. She never called me back.

A few days later, when I saw her, she was sweeping the street. "Hey!" she cried excitedly. "My excellent husband arrived just in time."

I hugged Saraswati and introduced her to my mother, in town for a visit.

Saraswati hugged and kissed my mother, too. "Your daughter is my good friend," she said. My mother, not easily moved to affection, was charmed by the embrace of such a vivacious woman.

"You must come see the baby," Saraswati sang, ushering us into her tidy house and seating us on the plush velveteen sofa below a gallery of Hindu gods.

Her little daughters flitted about like fairies while she ordered them in French to settle down. The lovely baby lay sleeping in his crib. All the children were fairer than their "black chicken" mother. The boy was fairest of all.

Saraswati handed me the infant.

"What's his name?" my mother asked.

"Marvin," Saraswati beamed.

"Marvin?" my mother repeated incredulously. She had few inhibitions, a characteristic now exaggerated by age. "You named your baby, Marvin?"

"Perhaps, we chose strangely," Saraswati admitted.

Mother nodded sympathetically. "Can you use his middle name?"

Something unpronounceable was mumbled in Sanskrit. "Marvin is my father-in-law's name," she explained. "He is an excellent man."

Later, I mentioned to mother that her comment might have hurt Saraswati's feelings. "Marvin, the baby's name is Marvin?" I imitated her perfectly.

"It was an honest response," she smiled.

Indeed, I understood the range and velocity of that honesty. It had fueled a list of grievances about my skin, hair, clothes, and friends. Especially skin.

"The sun will turn you swarthy," mother uttered with contempt. "Swarthy" like "black chicken" prompted me to go far away and never return.

The Dancing Shoes

Every week, Elaine and I were driven to dancing class by Noble
(her grandmother's chauffeur). He drove us in a Fleetwood Cadillac, spit-polished and waxed, from the outskirts of Buckhead to
The Temple, the oldest, most reformed and prestigious of Atlanta's
synagogues (founded in 1867), domed and columned (like Monticello), and located on a flourishing section of Peachtree Street near
the city's most elegant churches.

For dancing class, my mother bought me a brown velvet dress
with a scalloped lace collar and a pair of matching Capezio flats. It
was a fussy, childish outfit that would never attract the attention of
Terry Vatz, the only handsome (and pimpled) boy in the class. His
pimples gave him allure, making him look sexy and mature. The
DA haircut was a sign of rebel, and his black pegged slacks showed
off his slippery hips as he spun Miriam Blum around. I desperately
envied Miriam who wore slinky dresses. The best dressed were the
best dancers, and I was neither.

Noble drank as he drove from a flask that he said was filled with
root beer. We sat next to him, inhaling Wild Turkey. During dance
class while he waited, he proceeded to get loaded. One evening he
asked us, "Y'all know about nookie?"

"No!" we chorused, holding our breath and waiting for enlightenment.

"I gets fired for telling y'all," he slurred. "All I gonna say is if y'all don't know now, gonna know someday."

As soon as we reached Elaine's house, we raced to the dictionary. We searched for nookie, nukey, knooky, and other variations. The word itself connected to the mysteries of Terry Vatz's hips and Noble's promise of *someday*.

By the end of the year, Elaine and I had mastered the fundamentals of ballroom dancing: jitterbug, fox trot, waltz, and cha-cha-cha. Now we were ready to attend The Temple's teen dances in the fall.

I begged mother for a new, sophisticated, grown-up dress. That was a hopeless request. I consulted with my cousin, Peggy, guru of fashion. She had a dozen party dresses she wore when she dated college boys. She said I could borrow any dress I wanted.

The lavender satin sheath had a deep sweetheart neckline and cap sleeves. I took her gold heels (half-size too big) and a boxy gold evening purse, too. Peggy showed me how to sweep up my hair in a French twist and smudge my eyelids with lavender shadow. She lent me a Merry Widow and a white rabbit fur cape.

The night of the dance, I put on my brown velvet dress and velvet flats. "What a pretty picture!" my mother cooed. She made me turn and twirl. "At least, you won't look like a slut," she said.

At Elaine's house, I metamorphosed into a womanly package. When Noble arrived, he concurred. His eyes rolled up and down my stockinged legs. For the first time, Elaine and I sat in the back of the Cadillac.

The hall behind the sanctuary was crowded with teens. Everyone in the young set looked nervous except Terry and Miriam. They were in control. When the music started, he winked at her, and they spun, hip to hip, over the dance floor.

Our instructor tapped Sandy Weber (older by two years) for the first dance and pulled him out into the center. When the music stopped, she led Sandy to me. I was terrified, but when he held out his hand for Belafonte's "The Banana Boat Song," I followed him.

"Step, one-two-three," my lips commanded and feet followed. Soon, I stopped counting. I melted into the music. After three dances with Sandy, I kicked Peggy's gold heels into a corner.

At evening's end, the instructor dimmed the lights for the last dance. The lubricated chords of Johnny Mathis soared. Terry and Sandy each tugged on my hand. Choosing between them would prove emblematic of my romantic future: danger and desire versus loyalty. I chose Sandy.

Limping barefoot from the hall, I rested on Elaine's arm, strands of French twist falling, stockings ruined, my cousin's lavender dress stained, the rabbit cape askew. It had been the sweetest night of my life.

Noble jumped from the car to open the door, grunting happily (no doubt, anticipating we'd soon be drinking Wild Turkey with him).

Late that night, a bomb exploded at The Temple. Part of the sanctuary building was blown out. No one was hurt, but that was the only good news.

"They bombed The Temple!" my panicked mother called in the morning. "They bombed it!"

"Bombed?" I repeated in disbelief. "Why?"

"Negroes," she said. "It's because of Negroes."

A few hours later, my family went to The Temple. Hundreds of bystanders were on the street and sidewalk, viewing the damage. We had to pass through a ring of policemen. As the rabbi, in his dark robe, stepped onto the bema, the human buzz in the sanctuary grew absolutely silent.

"We are here," the rabbi said. He asked us not to be deterred by threats of violence. He likened the Negro struggle to that of the Jews, and the color line of segregation to the Red Sea.

I stared at the cavernous hole, praying that whoever planted the bomb would be sucked into the middle of the earth. Their hate scared me more than anything. I knew it firsthand. I had seen the parades of the KKK, marching by Leb's (Atlanta's large downtown Jewish delicatessen). Marching were girls and boys (all ages), dressed in white robes and conical hats, their eyes burning "Jew! Jew! Jew!" on my forehead.

After services, we filed outside and talked with other families on the sloping lawn. Terry, Miriam, Sandy, Elaine, their families stood nearby.

"What if the bomb exploded during the dance?" Miriam's mother wept into a handkerchief.

"Sue," a voice called over to me.

I turned to see my dance instructor. She was walking towards me with Peggy's gold heels.

"They were blown out the door by the explosion," she said.

"They aren't hers," my mother replied. "We've never seen them."

I took the shoes by their straps and skipped ahead to the parking lot.

"Noble!" I tapped the glass, leaned through the window, and shoved the shoes under his seat. I sent him a pleading look and ran to our car.

"You don't have to talk to Negroes like that," my mother reprimanded. "Up close like he's your friend."

"Marguerite, please," my father said.

"It's the reason for the bomb," mother insisted. "Jews and Negroes, they think we're the same."

My father leaned into my ear and whispered, "Garbage."

"That's the reason," my mother sobbed. "That's the reason."

The Red Beret

In the lobby of the movie theater, I hung (invisible) by my cousin, Peggy, watching the boys watch her. I had nothing to do except fidget with my purse and wait for someone to notice me.

"Y'all know my cousin, Sue, don't you?" she declared proudly.

Peggy's boys turned. Dutifully, they assessed my figure and face. However, no amount of primping had imparted any shred of sex appeal to me.

"Everyone says she'll be beautiful someday." *Someday* made it sound like I existed only in the future.

The blue darkness of the theater was a kind of war zone. Boys, single and in pairs, hovered and roamed. Young romance imploded. Couples split up and changed partners halfway through the show. Expletives and threats were shouted. Fist fights broke out. Cups, wrappers, popcorn, and ice were tossed around. Paper debris was everywhere.

Peggy assumed a royal seat in the center of the chaos, her favorite suitors on either side. At the far end of the row on the aisle, I sat next to one of the leftovers, a boy marked by ineptitude at sports, a boy who wore glasses.

From a distance, I witnessed their fealty to Peggy. I saw how she had to be gracious. She had to smile and laugh while I wasn't required to be anything. I was relieved of all feminine duties. I could ignore the commotion, observe without being disturbed, and know I had been spared.

Once Lenox Square was built, no one went downtown to shop. Ding Ho's (Atlanta's only Chinese restaurant) and Frohsin's (an elegant dress shop) were the only two enticements. Sometimes to flaunt our independence, Peggy and I skipped the movies on Saturday afternoon and took the bus from Buckhead into the center of the city.

Much of downtown Atlanta was segregated: restaurants, movie theaters, hotels. But, as we walked farther south, we found blocks where the color line wavered. The throngs of sharply dressed brown men and women made it hard to tell whose city it was.

Our adventures were modest: a grilled cheese sandwich at Woolworth's, the lingerie department at Davison's where we fondled nightgowns and slips, the white marble Carnegie Library (a miniature Parthenon) with its permanent tribute to Atlanta's most famous writer, Margaret Mitchell, and the highlight, a trick and magic shop which was a wedge-shaped room in a wedge-shaped building (I was a big fan of practical jokes, especially invisible ink). It was there our excursion ended unless Peggy could be persuaded to play a game of my own invention.

Peggy was reluctant. She usually made excuses to go home. Unlike me, she was not fascinated by the unknown. Her interests lay in controlling the familiar.

The game began the instant I chose. "Her!" I pointed.

Off we went, steadily following the figure ahead, traveling deeper into downtown, passing pawnshops and bars, surplus stores and resident hotels where wet clothes fluttered in the windows.

The sauntering, mocha-cream giantess was extraordinary. She sported a red beret no bigger than a doily, attached with black bobby pins to a coil of yellow hair. Her jacket was red leather, and her tight skirt had a slit that went above the knee. Under the contour of skirt, her backside jiggled and swung. We watched with fascination.

"No girdle," Peggy said.

"She's French," I told her.

"A slut?" she asked.

"A dancer, look at her legs." I was already something of an expert on French dancers, having attended a performance of the Folies Bergère on a trip to Europe when I was ten.

"And her name?" Impressed by my omniscience, Peggy inquired.

"Francine, Francine Monet." I had visited Giverny, too.

Mademoiselle Monet swayed through the crowd, leading us into the plumb center of Atlanta, a point not so much somewhere as nowhere, an empty spot where everything dropped away. When we walked out of this center, the city reformed itself into towers of tall, friendless buildings. Downtown was behind us. We had crossed into the quarter of pool halls, seamy hotels, taverns, and the Greyhound station where legless veterans sold No. 2 pencils.

"I'm not going there," Peggy cried.

Neither was Francine Monet. She walked on, leading us over a massive number of tracks into the railway terminal. This was another kind of center where people and histories waited and then disappeared.

We took up a position behind two pillars in the waiting room. Above us was the schedule board, times and destinations marked in chalk. Francine Monet checked the board, took a seat, removed a hand mirror from her purse, adjusted her perky beret, and by angling her mirror caught my eye like flint.

"She knows," I gasped.

"What?" Peggy jumped.

"That we're here."

We grabbed each other's hands, waiting for the next move. Hers, no doubt. We were no longer masters of the game.

She rose and exited the station, and like zombies, we followed her out the huge doors, past the taxi stand to a covered alley, piled high with luggage wagons and rusty boxes.

"Hey, girls!" Francine shouted at us.

"She speaks English," Peggy said. Even I was surprised.

We stood at the entrance to the alley, ready to run at any moment. She stood a few yards inside.

"Is this what you looking for?"

In one quick motion, she yanked up her skirt. There was neither girdle nor panties but a great deal of something else. Two white striped straps framed a bulge, a knob, a hump. The skirt came down so quickly that later, neither of us could believe what we saw.

Peggy and I bounced backwards. We raced past the station into downtown. Towers, movie palaces, department stores flashed above us. Brown people laughed and waved as we ran. Finally, we were on the bus, heading to Buckhead where there was time for the second show.

Do Clothes Make the Man?

A man, swaddled in loose white clothes, bronzed from the sun, his long blond hair tied up in a topknot, sat on a grassy knoll in Berkeley's south side Ho Chi Minh Park, dreamily playing his flute. He played it well, sitting cross-legged and holding the divine instrument to his lips like a portrait of Krishna on the frieze of a temple.

In the park one day, swami nodded in my direction. I nodded back (as if I had been chosen). With a graceful wave of fingers, he beckoned me to his spot. His gestures, his music which wafted as gently as a birdsong, and as I came closer, his blue eyes (as blue as humanly possible) proved hypnotic. He invited me to sit beside him. He played to me. After he finished, he slipped his flute into a plain white pillowcase which he used to carry all his instruments (saxophones, clarinet, piccolos, silver flutes, and shakuhachi) back and forth from the town to the hills.

"You live in the hills?" I asked. I was skeptical. Berkeley is divided between the hills and flats. Class divides along the same lines.

"Would you like to visit?" his blue-burning eyes pierced my cranium. "Although you won't be able to find it alone."

What I soon discovered was Jason literally lived in the hills. That is, within the perimeter of Tilden Park in a pup tent camouflaged with bunch grasses, branches, and eucalyptus bark. He ate only uncooked food so meals were not a problem. He transported his supply of dried fruit, nuts, sprouts, and water from the co-op in the flats up to his camping spot. Liberated from roof and walls, he lived like a nomadic prince on magnificent public land.

During the rainy season, he rented a room in a house near campus, but when the weather was fine, he preferred to live outdoors. Soon, I saw Jason's city room as well. Aside from a mattress on the floor and a stereo, it was filled, wall to wall, with LPs of jazz and Indian music.

Not only a musician, Jason was also a practitioner of Tantric yoga. My familiarity with Tantric was limited to a book of paintings, colors and shapes that looked related to Josef Albers rather than holy inspirations from the Himalayas.

"Tantra," Jason explained, "was a spiritual practice devoted to sex." He volunteered to be my spiritual guide.

First, I had to learn the basic principles of the practice. There were many. It was hard to keep track. The most important pertained to ritual bathing, ritual breathing, ritual visualization of colors, and sustaining sexual pleasure as long as possible. As our practice evolved (that is, having lots of sex), Jason informed me of additional principles. There were always new prescriptions and prohibitions. Whether invented on the spot, I could not say.

Although not listed in the Tantra's how-to handbook, Jason smoked pot continuously. He considered the pot medicinal, used to mask the pain from a car accident that broke his back. At sixteen, he was delivered dead to a hospital, and his mother's prayers brought him back to life. Jason came from a lineage of evangelist preachers on one side of Dallas, but love of reefer and jazz took him to the other side. When we went to hear Charlie Mingus, we had a front table at Keystone Corner where he and Charlie communed through vibes of mutual respect and understanding. Jason was a master musician, stoned in the hills.

For a few months, his enthralling spell was upon me. When the baby was with his father, he persuaded me to sleep out, not in his tent but inside a redwood tree trunk, a trunk hollowed out by lightening with an opening large enough to crawl in. We spread out a blanket and enjoyed the most spectacular private viewing of lights, bridges, and expanses of water and sky.

We camped at hot springs, north and south. We hiked in the hills. We feasted on dates and cheese. He played his flute, and I danced barefoot. It was a simple, pleasure-filled time. Even G-O-D visited me one night as a black box like a square in a Tantric painting.

My neighbor, Betty, asked me about the new man, lurking at all hours in the yard. She said he looked vaguely familiar.

When she was a student at Berkeley, walking from home to class, she once passed a man, leaning over a balcony and playing a flute. Playing it well. Naturally, the music attracted her. As she looked up, he looked down and beckoned her (with a wave of his enthralling fingers). She had no idea how to explain the hypnotic state that came over her, but she climbed the steps, entered a stranger's apartment, lay down on a bed, and let him make love to her.

He told her then (as he later told me), "I was born to give women pleasure."

"It's the same man," I assured her. The flute, the fingers, the singular purpose.

"In a different outfit," we concluded. What attracted women then was different now. Swami was in, hippy out.

As the number of Jason's rules increased, I grew rebellious and claustrophobic. I preferred sleeping indoors in a rectangular room on a bed. I preferred eating cooked food. I was tired of playing goddess. His insistence on pleasure wearied me. I wanted to return to a lowly, impure life.

We spent our last weekend at Geyser Hot Springs. On our way from the baths to the car, I stopped to talk to two young scientists embarked on experiments with the local water. After a short conversation, we walked on.

"Don't ever lift your eyes to another man," Jason threatened. Apparently, that was one of the rules.

I looked at him as if he might be joking. He wasn't. He was furious, nearly choking on rage. Instantly, two things became clear to me: he was a lunatic and I was in grave danger.

When we returned to Berkeley, I told him I couldn't see him anymore. He tried arguing. He tried sweet talk. He made promises, extravagant promises. He said he would give up Tantric yoga so we could have a child. Finally, he believed me and left me in peace.

A few years later, I saw Jason. He looked very different. He was wearing a denim suit (tailored slacks and blazer) and a cowboy hat. His face was wizened and hard. He was in town from Tampa where he worked for his uncle selling wigs. He said it was part of the Great Design. The next year, I received the sad news that he died in Florida of an overdose.

Occasionally, someone remembers that I knew him. They recall what an extraordinary musician he was. Whenever I hear the flute or drive by his field in Tilden Park, I send a little message to Jason, the man born to give women pleasure.

Parasols on the Palisades

The home on Ocean Avenue where Rob's father lived was an unhappy place. None of the resident relics smiled. They barely spoke. A old woman accosted me. "What do I do now?" she asked.

Relieved to cross the boulevard and walk along the Palisades, I encountered different old men, dozens of them, seated on folding chairs at folding tables, playing cards under the palms. Others, both men and women, were nearby, reading, knitting, noshing, gaming, and discussing subjects in several languages with great animation. They were also strolling with parasols on the cliffs of the Pacific in outmoded linen suits and long, print dresses. From the edge of the park, they could watch children, surfers, and sunbathers (young, reckless, and strong) below on the beach, small and faraway, who had years to go before they grew old.

One man was singing beautifully as well as playing cards. I sat near him and closed my eyes so I could listen. The breeze carried his voice closer and farther, picking it up like a signal from another world. The melody was Jewish, mournful, and distantly familiar. Perhaps, my grandfather, who used to tell stories to Peggy and me, had also sung it.

Once I had a great-uncle, "your great-great-great uncle," grandpa would say. We no longer remember his name, his occupation, his town. Or if he was wealthy or poor, learned or not. All we remember is the voice. He had a voice like a miracle. Once, he was captured by bandits who planned to kill him, but when they heard him sing, they let him go.

Suddenly, the voice stopped. The man rose from the table. He shook his white hair, grown past his shoulders, grinned, and filled his pockets with his winnings. Then, he nodded good-bye. His nods were singular, to each of his companions in turn. The three losers watched as he nimbly strode across the grass, his baggy linen trousers billowing behind him like sails.

I left my place on the lawn to follow, quickly catching up and walking by his side. At the red light we stood, waiting together, observing the traffic on Ocean Avenue, the cars slowly going home in the early hours of Sunday evening.

"Do you know me?" his voice startled me.

"I don't think so," I said.

"I thought perhaps you recognized me."

"I recognized your song," I said shyly.

The man's eyes glistened with a kind of cunning. "It's an old song, much older than me. Do you know how old that is?"

I nodded solemnly, thinking of my grandfather who walked halfway across Europe.

"How would a spring chicken know such a song?"

"I dreamt it," I told him

"At my age," he replied, "all life is dreaming."

By now, we had traveled east of the Pacific, passing Santa Monica's tidy, well-trimmed lawns, its spotless sidewalks, and shuttered houses. Nothing was out of place.

"The story of the song is the story of a good thief." He hummed a few bars.

I stopped walking and closed my eyes. Transported to a dusty path bordered by lime trees, I saw the vast red-streaked Russian sky, the wheat fields and orchards, the countryside where distances between estates and towns were calculated in versts. In long Russian novels, the number of versts had mystical correspondence in my mind to the number of pages.

"What would a good thief steal?" He interrupted my reverie.

"A cow for one's mother? An egg for one's child?" I had visions of Chagall's paintings populated with thieves.

He shrugged, "The thief steals a voice."

Better than cows and eggs.

"From the devil," he whispered, as if it were still a secret.

"The thief must have been brave," I said.

"Clever," the old man tapped his head. Strands of his hair like corn silk fell aside.

"And then what?"

"The devil couldn't speak or sing. The devil was mute for a long time."

"And?" I wondered.

The man spread his fingers as if the answer were obvious. "The devil never found him."

"Was he dead?"

"Quiet," the man said softly. "Very quiet, that's the only way to beat the devil." He laughed and dipped his head as he had done with his card partners.

I dipped mine and stuck out my hand. He stroked it like a rabbit, slowly blinking his lapis lazuli eyes. "Like a mystery," he sang. "The days are numbered, but we don't know what the number is."

Hazards of Dry Cleaning

June wanted to know why I suddenly looked so good. "Like a young girl," she said.

I was bashful to admit my good fortune. Already, it was a burden. Already, it had been met with skepticism and envy. "I have fallen in love," I confessed softly.

June's face lit up as she regarded my figure, my outfit, and smart, new haircut. A shower of additional compliments issued forth. June was happy for me. Embarrassed, I took my leave.

As weeks passed, June continued to be happy for me. June's enthusiasm did not wane. Whenever I dropped off or picked up, June inquired about a wedding date, his rapport with my children, whether my rush for the blouse coincided with travel plans. I grew weary of repeating that things were still going well.

Desperate to take back my privacy, I tried another cleaners. Predictably, the results were unsatisfactory. June's was the best cleaners in town.

I worked at looking less happy. I appeared pressed for time. With shoulders stooped and eyes cast down, I put my soiled sweaters on the counter and consulted my watch. For a month or more, June and I exchanged only the most basic information: stain, starch, crease, fold.

Then, one afternoon when business was slow and I had dropped my guard, June leaned across the countertop and asked me, "Don't I deserve to be loved, too?"

She flung her head to the back of the shop, behind the glass partition where hundreds of garments, each testimony to her hard work, hung inside their plastic wrapping waiting to be claimed. There, I spied June's husband at an ironing board. Although once gainfully employed as a civil servant, it now appeared he worked as his wife's assistant. His face had an aggressive, hang-dog look that said he had often strayed and looked forward to straying again.

Anger flushed June's face. She confided that her husband was unfaithful. He flaunted his affairs. His lovers called him at home. He beat their children. She wanted to divorce him and seek love, too. If only there was a way to prevent the state from giving him half of the business she had sacrificed to build. Most of all, she wanted to know if what worked for me would also work for her.

I glanced at the husband. "You're so pretty," he once uttered to me, lifting a hair from the front of the sweater I was wearing. After years of patronizing their business, I had never asked his name.

I held June's hand, admonishing myself for my little boast of happiness.

Now, it was my turn to pester her. Our talk no longer concerned my fullness but her distress, apparent in her disheveled clothing and uncombed hair. She rarely smiled. She told me she often spent nights in the back of the shop.

To comfort her, I took to complaining. I told her I was exhausted from my job, my teenager, and despite its loveliness, the demands of my relationship.

From time to time, my boyfriend accompanied me to June's. The story of her affairs depressed him. He had no interest in a personal relationship with a laundress. He preferred to wait outside.

After one of his shirts was ruined at his cleaners, I counseled him, "Go to June."

The next weekend, we arrived with a bundle of his clothes. June came from behind the counter and greeted him like a member of her family.

"A happy congratulations!" she beamed.

As she stepped forward, he stepped back, and without a word, dropped the shirts and tossed a winter jacket on top.

June retreated to count and separate the shirts, check the collars and cuffs, inspect the jacket, and mark the stains. When she handed him the claim ticket, he left brusquely.

"He doesn't sleep well," I apologized.

June patted my hand in sympathy. "Maybe, he'll feel better tomorrow."

The Spring Coat

Winter in Atlanta was not signaled by temperature or the occasional snowflake but by my mother wearing a fur coat. She had two. A day fur that was spotty, sporty, boxy, and fun to throw over pants and drive to the grocery store. And a night fur which was altogether different. It was blond mink and couldn't be tossed around. It was sacred.

I grew up relieved that real winter was elsewhere. Up north and out west. Whatever might be called a cold snap was only passing through. That meant when I left for college a thousand miles to the northeast, I was completely unprepared. A few weeks of autumn chill tested the limits of a wool blazer and padded car coat. By October's end, I couldn't bear to go outside.

Cold was the kind of misery that insured future failure. The earliest settlers had made that all too obvious. Those who survived suffered permanent psychological damage. They left not only a legacy of meanness on the national psyche, but an entire population of blotched and shivering New Englanders.

I called home.

"Fur," mother advised. "How do you think animals get along?"

First, I tried the shops on Copley Square, sequestered on upper stories with elegant names scripted in gold on plate glass. "Used fur?" The clerks were aghast.

Downtown Boston was more promising with flop houses and bars where people drank all day. On the rack of a hospital charity store, I found the very thing I needed: sheared raccoon. Its ugliness called to me. It cost ten dollars and weighed ten pounds. When real winter fell like an instrument of torture, I was prepared. I wore the coat everyday and slept under it at night. It was a lifesaver.

As the months dragged on, the coat began to fall apart. Pockets ripped, and the rotten lining tore. I left one cuff as a souvenir in New Haven. The other, I flung from the eighteenth floor of a New York hotel.

In March, my mother wrote she was sending up a spring coat for my birthday. Something light for the change of season, an essential item for a wardrobe, which in her mind guaranteed that I'd marry well and monogram my towels.

March passed without a sign of spring. I continued to drag around my beast, my head a speck in a sea of voluminous fur. It snowed in April, and mother's gift was a painful reminder of temperate weather.

My only warm and unencumbered moments were afternoons spent with a Harvard senior, a thin-blooded, thin-skinned Southerner like me. The coat was large enough to wrap around us both. After a film on Brattle Street and a cheap dinner at Hayes Bickford, we spread the coat on his bed and rolled across it naked like infants.

When spring actually arrived, it was perfect. The sky was powder blue with cotton-ball clouds perched on the horizon. The thermometer registered something reasonable. A few eager types even wore sandals and shorts. All of Boston went outdoors to celebrate.

I unwrapped my spring coat from the tissue paper: lightweight wool and double-breasted, a navy and white hounds-tooth pattern with navy braid piping on the collar and cuffs. It fitted at the waist, flared at the hip, and four large, navy buttons seamlessly fastened the two halves.

I had a Sunday date: a walk along the river followed by bad Chinese food and a retreat to my boyfriend's room.

Downtown, I boarded a car to Cambridge. I took a seat and lovingly touched my coat. Before I opened my book, I peered across the aisle at a pair of girls dressed like tropical birds. I took in their heavy eyeshadow and snug blouses, the layers of crinoline under their skirts, and their stockings three shades too dark.

They took me in, too, inspecting my stacked Pappagallo navy pumps and sleek spring coat. They were dressed for trouble. I was attired to appear untouched. They were showing off their allure. I was hiding everything. They were sexual. I was neutered by fashion. And no matter how pleased they were with their appearance, it was clear to each of us that they looked poor and I did not.

As the MTA slowed for Central Square, the girls rose and stood at the door beside me. They patted their sprayed beehived hair and chorused, "Bitch! Bitch! Bitch!"

I stiffened.

The subway wheels echoed. "Bitch! Bitch! Bitch!"

We rocked our way into the station and stopped. As the doors opened, the taller girl balled her hand into a fist and slammed it down on my arm. One punch and they were gone.

Through the window, I watched them skitter on their spike heels across the platform, giggling and pointing back to the car where I sat, my tears spilling onto my beautiful spring coat.

Monkey Suit

After six weeks in the Yucatan, Simon and I hitched a ride from Merida with a lepidopterist who insisted on stopping every few miles (on dangerously narrow roads) to dash about with a net until he succeeded in trapping and pinning an exquisite specimen of butterfly. I watched as he exercised the superiority of our species, the principle (inspired by science and religion) that man will always have inferior beings to kill, eat, convert, and kick around.

Our trip transpired over a couple of days through backwater Mexican towns (Chable and Catazaja) filled with beggar children whose ingratiating smiles were dingy, black nubs. "Where are their teeth?" I asked with alarm. They had no proper teeth because during pregnancy their mothers had overdosed on antibiotics (available at pharmacies without a prescription along with codeine cough syrup, a favorite of gringos).

We arrived in Palenque, high in the Chiapan jungle. Our sole intention was a visit to the temples of the Mayans, and after spending a night at a local campground, we set out in the morning by foot. A friendly American couple in a VW van stopped and offered us a ride. They knew nothing about pre-Columbian splendor. We were equally ignorant of the crop of psilocybin mushrooms, flourishing in local pastures. When they dropped us at the ruins, they handed us a jar of honey dotted with discolored nubs (the size of children's teeth). Honey, I would discover, was the best way to preserve, disguise, and transport illegal mushrooms.

We trucked up the road on an unmarked path into the mist-drenched rainforest where a pyramid appeared in the clearing like an hallucination (who needed mushrooms?). The near vertical ascent up the temple steps was terrifying. Climbing down into the interior even more so.

An ancient guardian of the site, reminiscent of Charon himself, held me firmly with one twisted hand while he tapped the stones with his staff. The narrow passageway of steep steps was slick with humidity and haunted by gloom. We descended slowly into the deep tomb. Dating back to 222 BCE, the tombs beneath the pyramids (unearthed only in 1952) once contained giant pearls, jade and obsidian masks (since removed to the Chapultepec Museum in Mexico City).

Palenque was a small, off-route town, quickly familiar. In one of its two cafes, we met a young Mexican (dressed like a college student) who attached himself to us. "They're federales," he whispered, his eyes sweeping across everyone in the room. "They arrest mushroom hunters. You like mushrooms?"

We weren't sure. However, we agreed to drive with him into the countryside of rolling emerald-green pastures, violet mountains in the distance, fields enveloped by soft moist air, and a canopy of cloudless blue sky.

Around us, a herd of Brahmin cattle munched happily except for the silvery bull who eyed us sideways with a proud, wild look of dominance. Briefly, he let us admire him, then lowered his candelabra horns, and kept them lowered until we turned around.

We retreated to the far end of cleared land where pasture met rainforest. There was no shortage of clusters of small mushrooms, the color of twilight, cheerfully poking their caps above pods of steamy bovine feces.

It crossed my mind that our companion intended to arrest us, but instead he eagerly began to devour mushrooms (unwashed). We followed suit. Promptly, I was communing with even greener grass and ungulates whose language I now intimately understood.

We were there for hours. Or minutes? The light deepened, and time passed irrelevantly. Our only timepiece was an approaching storm which signaled late afternoon. The clear sky was swept from sight and replaced with masses of boiling black thunderheads.

As we rose to leave, it began to pour. Simon retrieved a plastic raincoat from a packet the size of a postage stamp. Our Mexican amigo pulled out a battered poncho. I, however, was thoroughly unprepared. Wrapped in a cotton house dress (purchased for a few pesos in Merida), browned the color of a raisin, barefoot, with long braids entwined with florescent weeds, I trudged behind the two well-equipped men.

Immediately, I was soaked. The thin cotton clung to me like tattooed skin. My face lifted to the warm rain. I opened my mouth and swallowed. I was deliriously happy (like a child) to be wet and surprised.

Remember the diagram of Man's Evolution? From ape to Homo sapiens? We were that picture of evolution. Blond, upright, and ever-prepared went first. Third-world brother trotted dutifully behind, ever second. And impervious to the downpour, I slipped backwards on a rain-soaked hillside that separated the divine emerald patches from the car.

In my state of enhanced consciousness, I identified with creatures who had not yet invented plastic raincoats. It would appear I had barely advanced beyond the moment when cousin Lucy climbed down from the trees.

—

From Palenque, we journeyed by bus to San Cristobal where we lolled around for a month, visiting remote Indian villages and scribbling profound thoughts in our notebooks.

We continued south to the Guatemala border. Like all foreigners (with long hair, blue jeans, and backpacks), we were suspected of conspiring with Che and subjected to a police search. Finally, we were allowed to cross. A rattling, smoking, crowded contraption carried us through the wondrous mountain landscape, jagged and compact. The indigenous highland peasant families, attired in glorious *huipiles*, traveled with us, getting off and on, with their livestock and large, loose bundles. Or standing by the road, frantically waving for the bus to stop as the driver indifferently sped by.

Our destination (along with other young vagabonds) was Panahachel on Lake Atitlan, surrounded by volcanic peaks and twelve small villages named for the Apostles. Warm days, cool nights, swims in the clear, deep volcanic lake. For pennies, we swung in a hammock hotel and feasted at the beach side vegetarian restaurant.

The earthly paradise was marred by bank guards with machine guns; oblivious hippies (especially men), sunbathing nude at the lake where the native women washed themselves (dressed in slips); Simon's egregious flirtations; the theft of my favorite jacket (red-wine velvet with a peplum and grosgrain frogs); and my own bouts of nausea.

We found Guat City filled with soldiers, foul smells, and indigents displaced from the impoverished countryside into sordid slums. On New Year's Eve, the military (in training for death squads) goose-stepped their way across the city's silent and deserted central square. No one was celebrating.

Night and day, my nausea increased, triggered by the smells of sewage and cilantro. I searched out a clinic, stumbled through a few words of elementary Spanish, and pointed to my belly.

They took a urine sample, and a few hours later when I returned, I was greeted by shouts from the clinica staff, "Positivo!"

"Positivo sí?" I had to clarify. "Or positivo no?"

"Positivo sí!" they cheered.

"Positivo con niño? Or sin niño?"

They embraced me, "Con niño! Con niño! Con niño!"

Not only nauseated, I was now ambivalent. Unmarried with few practical skills, I was in a complicated relationship, possibly alone, nearly broke, and far from home.

We turned around and headed north, stopping to rest in Oaxaca (where I was able to satisfy my craving for Corn Flakes); and again in Mexico City (where I was waited on by servants in the mansion of Simon's former student).

Two months later, as our train neared the US border, it separated (like a worm) in the middle of the night, his half wiggling its way towards Nogales, while I continued north to Tijuana. Buses, trains, cars. I only wanted to lie down and curl up.

—

I was totally unprepared to start a new life in California. I had a hundred dollars cash, a small sum of travelers' cheques, and the address of a friend in the Haight-Ashbury who let me settle on her couch.

During my first week in San Francisco, I made my way to Union Square, the city's elegant epicenter. Ten years earlier, my mother and I visited the city for the first time, shopping at I. Magnin, having our hair styled at Vidal Sassoon, dining on Nob Hill. Now, my hair hung in braids to my waist, and I dressed in second-hand *huipiles*, dyed in coffee by the Maya to cover the stains of wear.

The American Express office was not far. I submitted a claim for traveler-cheque theft (valued at $500). The clerk processed the order for replacement and informed me that the new cheques would be available at the end of the day.

By noon, I had qualms. I didn't want to start my new life with a new baby in a new place with a scam. I returned to American Express and stammered to the clerk, "It was a mistake. A friend took the cheques."

"You said 'stole,'" she recalled, reaching for another set of forms. Apparently, I would now be required to press charges.

"May I speak to your supervisor?" The question of choice when all else fails.

"I don't want them!" I cried as I confessed my pregnancy, my marital status, my lack of resources, and my impractical liberal arts education. The supervisor listened sympathetically. He would not call the police.

Outside again, I was elated to have avoided both crime and punishment. With the guidance of a friend and the largesse of the State of California, I was soon provided with food stamps, medical care, and a modest monthly sum.

Despite the emotional love storms (whipped up by Simon blowing in and out of town), I grew into a fat, contented animal. A fondness for my primate cousins was confirmed. I looked to them to remind me that existence itself contains all meaning.

—

I settled into a cheap flat in Oakland. For a short while, Simon settled in with me. My two closest neighbors were also pregnant. Every morning, we met to walk (slowly) and talk (distractedly) about our strange physical sensations, our weird frightening dreams, and our misshapen bodies performing at peak.

I was invited to appear in a pregnant pin-up calendar. When the photographer asked if I had any nude fantasies, I suggested he photograph me in my 1957 Chevy wagon. I thought it was a classic, but for March, he selected a shot of me collapsed in a rocking chair. The collapse was no exaggeration. I was nearly three weeks past due.

The evening I went into labor, I had spent the day at Muir Beach, lying immobilized on the sand. In fact, Simon had to push me up the flight of steps into our flat (he couldn't have possibly carried me).

Labor started while I was playing cards in the kitchen with my midwife. For several hours, the contractions were bearable. When they grew unbearable, I hunched naked on my knees on a mattress on the floor, my posterior lifted in the air. Embarrassment briefly prevented me from groaning. But embarrassment, along with other inhibitions, vanished.

Once I began to utter animal sounds, I felt better. The midwife accompanied me. Together, we moaned and groaned for hours. By dawn, I was convinced the baby was about to be born. I was wrong. Seven more hours were to pass before the wet, bloody, mucous-covered creature was spit out between my legs onto the floor.

The baby lay on my chest, and thankfully, I lay on a bed with clean sheets. From time to time, I yearn to recall the animal sensations of pregnancy, childbirth, and nursing, long engulfed by the troubles and pleasures of child-rearing. Occasionally, I find their reawakening in the pictures of apes whose expressions look familiar while all around me is a world of human strangers.

White-Collared

At first, I worked like a plow horse. I stayed late. I volunteered for extra assignments. Although unaccustomed to getting up early, battling traffic, and fretting over proper business attire, I was happy to have a job.

By week six, my fatigue had resolved, but everyday ended with a headache. All day, I squinted at the computer. The work aggravated my eyes. Not only did I need a screen shield from the computer glare and overhead florescent lights, I also called for an appointment for glasses.

Month three, my nasal passages ran like a sewer. I sneezed, wheezed, coughed, and spewed all day. "It's normal," my manager said, assuring me I would soon adjust to the poorly ventilated building.

During week ten, my scalp started to itch. I couldn't stop scratching. I suspected lice, contracted from the kids, but the diagnosis was severe dandruff from stress. The doctor prescribed tar shampoo and a metal comb.

By the fourth month, I had some relief. For a few days, I actually felt well. Then, one morning, I awoke with a pain between my atlas and armpit. I couldn't raise my arm above my elbow. A purse strap was unbearable. Sleep was only possible with a heating pad and pillow to hoist my torso. In short, I was crippled. I took high doses of anti-inflammatory drugs and made appointments to see a physical therapist, acupuncturist, and spiritual advisor.

Twenty-four weeks on the job, fatigue, stuffy head, neck tension, and dandruff were behind me. However, for a split second every quarter-hour, I gasped for air. I assumed it was anxiety over a deadline, but the deadline passed, and the breathlessness did not. Eventually, this malady simply subsided, and I inhaled at a normal rate.

In my seventh month, I was really managing. A paycheck came reliably every two weeks. Medical benefits were secure. The children had grown accustomed to afternoons without me. In fact, the days were fine. It was the nights that were untenable. Nightmares!

As one ailment resolved itself, it was replaced by another, more ominous than the predecessor. Hydra had reared her ugly heads, and they were all inside my own.

I didn't have to look far for the cause. No doubt, the building was designed by a sadist. The ceilings were low and the few window slits reserved for a dozen executives. The interior walls, industrial carpeting, desks and file cabinets were uniformly battleship gray. Privacy was a ludicrous concept in the tiny cubicles that served as offices. Taps, buzzes, grinds, hums, burps, nail clippers, coughs, curses, and conversations dispersed into the open space above us. Sadly, even filled with human noise, the atmosphere was profoundly lifeless.

Our building, located in a premiere industrial park, had paved over the premiere agricultural acreage that had once thrived with orchards. Traveling a few blocks in any direction led to four identical mini-shopping centers, each with a grocery store, a restaurant of ethnic cuisine, an athletic shoe store, and a nail salon.

Inside my half-portion of cubicle, I tried beautification. I stuck my children's drawings and a poem by William Blake on the carpet-like wall. Other employees also exhibited their personal touches, recalling who they were and informing everyone else who they might be if they didn't have to work at the Data Center. Our efforts reminiscent of rituals in which the dead are buried with their prized possessions.

In my ninth month, I was pleased to report all signs of physical ailments had eased and nightmares ceased. I had successfully joined the American workforce.

—

My next job was more convenient. I didn't have to drive on freeways or worry about what to wear. No one complained if I left early. If the kids were sick, I could lay them on a pallet on the office floor. Although I was not paid much, I preferred being close to home.

When a lawsuit forced the company to cut back staff, I received a pink slip, indicating income and health insurance were now terminated. Pointlessly, I remained in my office, tidying, emptying, dusting, packing. Most of all, I was waiting for a reversal of fortune. By closing time, the position of telemarketer had been rejected by six other employees. I was next in line.

Whatever the job at hand, I exceeded expectations. Management found me cheerful and capable. During the second round of layoffs, the new Mr. President informed me he had personally saved my job.

"Personally," he emphasized.

Now, it was understood I owed him. Payback came a week later when he asked if I had time to help him pick out a suit at Nordstrom's Semi-Annual Men's Sale.

"I never make the right decisions when it comes to clothes," he smiled sheepishly. "My wife always chose them for me." He was in the middle of a divorce.

I found the courage to be blunt. I did not hold back. Shopping for men's clothes was not in my job description. I had children to attend to after work. I couldn't spare the time. In the next round of layoffs, I expected to lose my job. As it turned out, Mr. President lost his.

—

At the new job, there were just two of us. "My one and only" was how Herr Director described me to his astrologer. Our office was a renovated Victorian storefront a few blocks east of San Francisco Bay. We worked for a non-profit that did good work. Beware! The last time I was hired by a non-profit (an organization like David v. Goliath that battled nuclear arms), I was tyrannized and belittled by my celebrated humanitarian boss.

In the new job, Herr Director used au courant terms like "non-hierarchical" and "empowerment" to let me and everyone else know he was not really a boss. He was a facilitator, guide, expediter, and friend. Although I did ninety percent of the work, whenever it was successful, he took the credit, and with his smooth, sententious manners, made us all feel gloriously connected to the process. His favorite pastime was spouting ideas. They were as prolific and ephemeral as gas and erupted every time he stopped by the office on his way out for a latte.

The only time his casual, slovenly style (rooted as much in numerology as policy reform) reversed dramatically was the day before our monthly board meeting. Then, he was inspired to rush around, preparing reports, his mood altering from carefree to cruel.

He did work hard at pleasing the board. He briefed them on the positive trends of the organization, convinced them to volunteer for the tasks of his job, and adroitly redirected the conversation to his latest getaway plans with a sweetheart. The board (all men) loved him. They wished they had jobs that were open-ended and girlfriends instead of wives.

When I first encountered Herr Director, he had a small grant. I needed a job, and he needed a feasibility report. He hired me to write it. After he got a bigger grant, he took me on as a part-time employee with flexible hours and a flexible work plan. Naturally, I appreciated the flexibility, short hours, and casual dress code. While I was initially relieved there was no boss breathing down my collar, I soon realized there was no boss. Period.

My job title was project manager. Basically, I was hired to wipe up Herr Director's messes, shepherd broken agreements and abandoned clients, and in case he was working out at the Y, perform reconstructive surgery. Since the single organizational project was complex, I deemed it prudent to handle all the particulars myself, assigning a few remedial tasks to Herr Director.

He was perfectly receptive to the arrangement. His astrologer told him I wouldn't make trouble as long as he remembered to thank me. Everyday, he called in with heartfelt thanks and once a month, brought me flowers.

Finally, I exploded. I said we should re-evaluate the workload. He agreed. I should be paid on time. He agreed. I should get a bonus for the half-million dollar grant I successfully pursued. He agreed. But after all the harmonious agreeing, nothing changed. Workload, pay schedule, bonus, the arrangement remained the same.

After Herr Director rented a house at the beach, it became inconvenient for him to commute. When he did turn in a rare guest appearance, it was either to recount woman troubles or spiritual progress with Herr Guru. I rarely discussed personal matters, and Herr Director rarely discussed work. According to him, the guru's teachings must have taken hold, for the project was shaping up nicely.

After Herr Director exhausted his treasure trove of spiritual anecdotes, he engaged our office mates in chitchat, made a couple of phone calls, followed by a leisurely meal and long walk. Although I prepared him a list of simpleton assignments, he didn't do them. Not because he couldn't but because he preferred not to. Like a philandering husband, he was busy having fun while the wife watched the kids.

Fun, he pursued like a zealot. To him, we were co-conspirators in his good times. I got the opportunity to work, and he got the opportunity to pay himself for goofing around. He was the prodigal, gifted rascal, and I was the anxious caretaker. He was the relaxed husband, I the overworked wife. I was the project manager, and he was the director, out to lunch.

—

I had technical skills plus strong letters of recommendation. It was not difficult to find a new job where duties were the same and staff eerily familiar. Like the old job, a trans-sexual managed customer relations. The chief technician wore shirts with revolutionary slogans. The chief-of-sales brought in donuts on Monday and organized games of Frisbee tag on Friday. The petite women who ruled the design department at the new company were physically identical to the old: pony tails, oversized glasses, starched blouses. The shipping clerk was a skinny blond with a shag haircut, popcorn muscles, cutoffs, and Van Halen decals on his truck. Doppelganger to the owner of the former company, the new one was a handsome foreigner who wore custom-made silk suits and oversaw operations like the province his family owned in his Third World country of origin.

In fact, the new job was a phantom of the old. Everyday, I got up, dressed in the same consignment-shop clothes, packed the same lunches for the kids, drove to a job identical to what I used to do, and sat at a desk with the same plastic desk caddie.

I weighed coincidence with probability. Either, I had died in a car accident and been reincarnated as an office worker. Or if not dead, I might be functional but insane. Or perhaps, I was trapped in a warp where everything blended into a simultaneous time-space continuum.

My miserable mind was helpless, but my body knew what to do. I contracted serial maladies. I caught viruses. I was susceptible to allergies. I fell down the stairs and hurt my back. I was on official leave. When leave ended, I was officially laid off.

The day I received my final notice, I became whole again. Robust and fit. There was no end of wonderful things to do before the unemployment checks ended and I began looking for another job.

Sex Education

At the end of my tenth year, my mother solemnly ushered me into a dark corner and explained the mechanics of procreation. His thing into her thing, that was sex education. Fortunately, there were more stimulating clues around me, portents like 69 on STOP signs, men waving bananas from cars, couples rubbing each other on escalators, news of banned films from Atlanta's single art house, creased passages of books circulating at summer camp, and fornicating dogs, locked at an awkward juncture for a painfully long time. I studied these mysteries but remained baffled by their meaning. By the next year, bafflement had vanished. I received my first true lesson in sex education.

My informant was Lilly, the family maid, who spent five nights a week in a small room at the far end of our large dreary house. Lilly was beautiful, so beautiful it was painful to watch her sweep and iron. She should have been an African queen or movie star. At night, I would creep through the foreboding halls to her room.

"Lilly, can I come in?"

"Uh-huh," she grunted.

Lilly was resting from the day's work. She had removed her white uniform and folded it over the closet door. She lay immodestly in a slip and panties, stretched out on the narrow bed, curled in a beguiling repose, her straightened hair picturesquely arranged on the pillow, and her regard for me royally indifferent.

Tentatively, I took a worshipful seat at Lilly's feet. She spoke to me about this and that: her children in South Carolina, her boyfriend who was an Atlanta cop, her parents in a remote part of the state. She spoke to my ignorance.

While I listened, I stared at the fur covering her long and shapely legs. She didn't shave because her boyfriend preferred it otherwise.

"He loves feeling it," she told me. That was the sort of revelation I had been waiting for.

Sometimes, she lifted her hair and let me touch the pair of crescent scars on either side of her neck where her husband had "poked" her. The knife went in right and came out left. Her sister removed it. "It slipped out clean like a butter knife," Lilly said.

This too was evidence. Sex was tenderness of touch and terror of violence.

Lilly didn't stay long. When she left, I hoped her beauty had catapulted her beyond such meager circumstances. Her presence was transient, but the albums of Hank Ballard and the Midnighters were a permanent fixture. A destination of nightly visitations. I had a turntable, a stash of records, and privacy where I played "Annie Had a Baby" and "Sexy Ways" over and over, attempting to learn the language and decipher the code.

> Annie had a baby/can't work no mor'
> Annie had a baby/can't work no mor'
> Every time she starts to workin'
> Has to stop and walk the baby cross the flo'r
> Flo'r, flo'r, flo'r . . .

When I finally figured out that Annie had had a baby out of wedlock and worked as a prostitute, I thought I was a genius. These songs were thrilling, taboo at the least and likely criminal. I couldn't believe people wrote such audacious music, and I had the clandestine privilege of listening. It dared me to dream of desperation unlike any I had imagined.

By fourteen, I often went to hear Hank Ballard and the Midnighters. He lived in Atlanta and by decent people's standards, was considered a purveyor of "devil" music and an evil influence on children. My mother tried to forbid his records in our house, but it was way too late. I had memorized each lyric and unlocked the shibboleth of every song. More significant, the music now lived in my body.

Hank Ballard was the original Twist man. He wrote and recorded "The Twist" before Chubby Checkers turned it into an international craze. By then, Doug Clark and the Hot Nuts had invaded Atlanta and assumed supremacy in the universe of salacious music. They played all over the city, at downtown hotels and fraternity parties. Their personal popularity and record sales were generated exclusively by word of mouth because none of their songs ever made air-time. X-rated all the way, they were one of the most dynamic and ubiquitous dance bands of the era until they were banned from campuses and banished out of Dixie.

According to an homage to Doug Clark (who died in 2002), Richmond, Virginia passed a law in the early 1960s: NO HOT NUTS.

The chorus of their signature song was:

Hot nuts/hot nuts/get 'em from the peanut man
Yeah, yeah, yeah, yeah
Hot nuts/hot nuts/get 'em anyway you can.

"Get 'Em from the Peanut Man" is the title of an old blues song, but the Doug Clark version was simply called "Hot Nuts." Each verse described the color of a woman's dress and a sex act (something like the *Kama Sutra* of R&B).

See that girl dressed in black
She likes to do IT on her back.

IT was enough for me. IT was the ultimate. The Hot Nuts chorus yelled, "Yeah! yeah! yeah!" as we crowded around, growing wilder with each suggestion: red-bed, green-scream, pink-stink. For hours, dancing to "My Ding-a-Ling" and "Baby, Let Me Bang Your Box."

Exhausted and ecstatic, we headed into the night. My well-mannered date opened and closed the car door so I could climb in. Then, he carefully drove me home where I waited for him to walk around and again open my car door. Then, he extended his hand to help me from the car and escorted me to the front steps where we stood a few moments under the porch light. I thanked him and delivered a chaste kiss, wondering if that counted.

Baby Doll

In Atlanta, there were three Jewish social clubs with three improbable names: Progressive, Standard, and Mayfair. Although Jews were banned from clubs for Christians, they copied the same customs of exclusion, ranking the status of their membership by class and country of origin. Our grandfather was the first Ashkenazim invited to join the German-dominated Standard Club, a point of family pride for two generations.

On Sundays, our family usually dined at the club. Peggy and I grew accustomed to dressing up for dinner, sipping Shirley Temples at the bar, staining our fingers with the red shells of pistachios, and watching our grandmother play the slot machines. When we were older, we spent summers by the pool, either playing canasta or flirting with the attractive (gentile) lifeguards. I don't recall anyone swimming.

Except for bridge and booze, my father had no interest in club life. Conversations about real estate and golf depressed him. He took no interest in clothes or automobiles. He drove only my grandmother's discarded Cadillacs, and when he finally bought a new car, it was an unfashionable Rambler. His careless grooming and sloppy attire were a constant source of irritation to my mother who wanted him to look presentable.

"Is it so difficult to make an effort?"

Apparently, it was.

My father had been trained as a chemical engineer with a masters degree before the age of twenty. The smartest boy (poor) married to the most beautiful girl (rich) was the equation of our family legend. The household divided accordingly: intelligence signaled indifference to material things, and beauty narcissistically indulged in acquiring them.

Although daddy lacked business experience and ambition, he was asked after the war to join Puritan Mills. Club life and elegant home were part of the vice-presidential package along with dances in the ballroom on Saturday night and dinners on Sunday. He was a witty, garrulous man, but no one paid attention when he turned the conversation to foreign policy and the plight of Negroes.

"Relax and have a good time," his pals said. Like him, they had fought in the war. One had lost a leg, another an eye. They had already sacrificed. Now, they wanted to forget and enjoy life. If only Eddie Breen would let them.

By tenth grade, Peggy's prediction about me had come true. Overnight, I was a pretty girl. I went out as much as possible with any boy willing to drive to the edge of the city to pick me up. On weekends, I spent the night at Peggy's house where we often engaged in late dating: coming home at midnight with one boy and sneaking out later with another. She groomed me on clothes, cigarettes, sex, and subterfuge.

Unfortunately, there was no place to go for late dates except the Standard Club golf course with its smooth, mowed rolling greens under a sky lit by fireflies and stars. While the course overflowed during the day with men cursing short drives and poor putts, at night it was a deserted, enchanted place.

Enchantment was forever demolished when Bruce Perry (a young lifeguard) and I were discovered by the police on the seventeenth hole, Peggy and Charlie on the eleventh, and another couple outside the clubhouse (which had initiated the call to the police). We were charged with trespassing. Everyone was a college student except Peggy and me. Quickly, she assessed the danger of our juvenile status. We lied about our age. Instead of hauling us to jail, the police issued tickets and a court date.

"What are we gonna do?" I cried.

"Look innocent," Peggy said, sweeping my hair into a pony tail. "In baby-doll dresses, we can't look more innocent than that."

Our day in court arrived. Each of us (including Brenda, a sophomore at University of Georgia) was attired in a baby-doll dress with a square low-cut neckline, short puffed sleeves, a fitted bodice trimmed in rickrack, and a ballerina skirt to the knee. Any similarity among us ended at Brenda's bustline where the upper hemispheres of her enticing breasts jiggled like vanilla pudding.

We sat nervously in the back of the hot courtroom. It was packed with black youth arrested for pickpocketing and shoplifting. During the three hours of procedures, dozens of cases were heard. The judge pronounced everyone guilty.

We were terrified.

Finally, our case was called. We stood before the judge who peered at us over his glasses. "Trespassing at the Standard Club at two in the morning, correct?"

"Yes, sir," Peggy spoke up.

"Are your families members of the Standard Club?"

"Our grandfather, Morris Abelman, was invited to join in 1934," Peggy spoke again.

The judge smiled indulgently and stared at Brenda. "I understand y'all go to college?"

"Yes, sir," we said in unison.

"Duke," Bruce Perry added.

"And you?" the judge asked Brenda.

"Athens, sir," she responded, lifting the tip of her bosom so the jewels of her sorority pin could sparkle in the light.

"Dismissed," the judge pounded the gavel.

Outside in the molten parking lot, Brenda wiped the beads of perspiration from her face, adjusted her baby-doll neckline, and fluffed her skirt.

We were in awe of Brenda. She had saved us.

Mourning Crepe

Aunt Edith was a woman desperate to be loved, which led to affairs during her marriage and following her divorce, real and imagined. After decades of unhappiness, late in life, my aunt suddenly and mysteriously became happy, a happiness nearly impossible to conceive. Crankiness disappeared, drinking subsided, bitterness dissolved. She stopped concocting stories about rare and fatal diseases. She behaved civilly to everyone. A veritable childlike sweetness enveloped her existence.

On the other hand, my mother (her sister) continued to pester her doctors for poison pills. She rarely went out. She wore stockings with runs. She cut her own hair with cuticle scissors. Her YSL jackets were stained and her tennis shoes had holes.

The two sisters had not spoken in fifteen years, since an incident at my grandmother's deathbed when mother jumped on Edith like a beast, requiring three nurses to pull them apart. Afterwards, a traumatized Edith was hospitalized for shingles, which prompted her son, Malcolm, to threaten to kill my mother if she didn't leave his alone.

This sibling feud neither began nor ended with their mother or children. It started with a competition for their father's affection and eventually moved on to mine. Growing up, it was noteworthy that my father's attentions were often directed to my aunt who hung adoringly on every word.

During my parents' boisterous arguments, mother accused daddy of "screwing" her sister. These frequent, verbal attacks, accompanied by crystal, cutlery, and shoes, induced him to flee our house and pass the night in my aunt's guest room. No doubt, complaining of the madness at home.

Husbands of both sisters worked at my grandfather's mill. If Edith bought a luxury car or fur coat, mother made public denouncements at club dinners and private parties that her sister was stealing the family fortune. For years, they kept tabs on each other's purchases, vacation plans, house renovations, and charge accounts. Information gleaned from maids and sales clerks, willing to gossip for small tips.

Now in their seventies, it was reasonable they should reestablish a relationship. They were both alone with common memories of common dead friends, living in Atlanta on limited fixed incomes with identical laments about their long fall in the world.

During Aunt Edith's few happy months, the sisters occasionally went to a movie or lunch. Rapprochement ended when Edith accused my mother of stealing a set of silver dessert spoons. She claimed her ex-husband of thirty years was spreading rumors about her former infidelities. She refused to get out of bed, waited to be fed, and generally deteriorated from paranoia to delirious juvenile behavior.

As soon as Edith was diagnosed with dementia, my mother's own death wish faded away. Her new mission in life was to take good care of her sister. Although she bemoaned the waste of Edith's mind (publicly), the real loss lay in the demise of their lifelong rivalry.

The night before my aunt died, I dreamed I was in Atlanta at her bedside. "Aunt Edith," I said stroking her hand.

No response.

"Aunt Edith, it's Sue."

No response.

"Aunt Edith, you loved me, remember?"

Instantly, she sprang to life. Her eyes unglazed and looking straight at me, she said, "I hated you."

Even in my sleep, I had to laugh.

The next morning, I was called with confirmation of the news. Within a few hours, I had boarded an airplane and landed in the lushness of late spring in the South. Confetti blossoms of crepe myrtle dotted the avenues. Sunlight splayed the canopy over Aunt Edith's grave.

In attendance were three generations of slim, good-looking brunettes, wearing fashionable black suits. Mother was the most stylish in a dark silk sheath, a triple strand of large pearls, her head wrapped in point d'esprit. She sat amicably beside her nephew Malcolm in front of Edith's casket (despite their history of death threats and animosity).

After the interment, we meandered up the hill to the family plot bought by Morris Abelman for his daughters and their husbands. Sadly, Edith had to be buried elsewhere since the second wife of her deceased ex-husband (a blond convert from Mississippi and twenty-five years his junior) now had legal claim to the grave.

"Edith should have taken my space," mother cackled, pointing to the empty slot beside my father. "She was always trying to throw him into bed. Here, they could have slept together for eternity."

From the cemetery, we convened at mother's large Peachtree Street apartment where for several hours, we passed around the family photo albums, laughing and weeping over the fate of the bloodline.

A week after Edith's death, mother received a call from a stranger who had read the obituary in the newspaper.

The woman introduced herself as the daughter of Narcissus. Narcissus, long dead herself, had worked for my grandparents' household from 1923 to 1939. "Miss Marguerite?"

Mother must have smiled with pleasure. She had not been addressed with subservience in years.

"My mother loved Miss Marguerite and Miss Edith like her own," the daughter said.

Next to the phone rested a framed sepia portrait of the two young sisters in their organdy pinafores and barbershop bobs. They were lovely, pristine children with no clue of the desertion, suicide, and mental illness that would eventually dog them. On the contrary, they exuded the privilege of their birth and Narcissus' careful grooming.

"But she could never decide which one she loved more."

Psychic Shopper

Does the hook snare the fish? Or the fish swim up and grab the hook? Peter and I used to sit for hours with rod and bait, our legs dangling over the pier, sipping beer, waiting for something to happen. Most of the time, nothing did. But that didn't matter. We were looking for an excuse to do nothing and preferred if it had a name. Fishing is the best apology ever invented.

If I have an hour, not long enough for a walk but enough time to lose myself, I visit the local discount department store. There's no effort to make anything look attractive, and items are often one-of-a-kind. I prefer this ocean of discards and seconds to the tidiness of conventional retailers. Suspended in a meditative state, I scan the sad polyesterscape until I spot something lively, something made from natural fiber. I check the size (mine) and price (almost nothing): a DKNY linen skirt, a merino wool sweater, a pair of Italian leather sandals.

After trolling the clothes, I wander down aisles stuffed with towels, kitchen gadgets, and crockery. I pick up a few gifts: an oddball vase or a bib for a baby who hasn't been born. Like fishing, absent-minded shopping requires no concentration. It carries no expectations. It's an experience of detachment.

My cousin, Peggy, possesses rare telepathic instincts about clothing, confirmed by a holiday office party in 1999. The week before the occasion, she pictured exactly what she would wear (brown velveteen slacks and harlequin silk blouse). She drove to the discount department store. Voila! They were there, waiting as she imagined: her size, good quality, and affordable. She tested other items. On demand, a trench coat, summer loafers, and chiffon dress materialized. Dross to gold. Thought bubble to blazer.

Peggy consulted a friend with a small, successful home business. Together, they made a list of what she would need to launch Psychic Shopper.

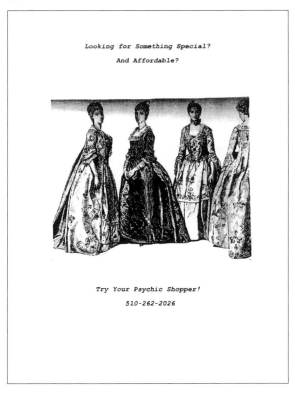

Looking for Something Special?

And Affordable?

Try Your Psychic Shopper!
510-262-2026

The same day that Peggy posted her flyers on utility poles, she got her first call.

"Psychic Shopper!" We had already spent an hour practicing her inflection.

"The stain won't come out!" a panicked woman cried. She had spilled coffee on the brocade suit she intended to wear to her son's wedding.

Peggy was calm and reassuring, speaking in a tone that invited confidence. "I'll need your age, weight, coloring, and height."

As Jackie Germaine replied, the picture of a tall, heavyset woman emerged: dark skin, shoulder-length dyed red hair, fifty-two years old, size 16.

"I see it," Peggy spoke from a trance. "Elegant but not dull, formal but not staid. I'll get back to you before Tuesday."

Three observations related to shopping:

- Size is rarely accurate (varies by manufacturer and style)
- Three is the maximum number the brain's shopping hemisphere can process
- Comfort (emotional & physical) for women over 40 (unless they're delusional) is the most persuasive factor

After they hung up, Peggy closed her eyes and let Jackie's body drift around. "Blue," she concluded. The following day, she brought home the possibilities: a navy, cotton lace suit, a turquoise sheath with a bolero jacket, and a rayon evening gown in divine Carolina blue.

When Jackie arrived, she overflowed with gratitude. She chose the evening gown and insisted that Psychic Shopper come to the reception.

"Gold," Peggy recommended. "Gold shoes, gold purse, gold pin. You'll look like King Tut's mother."

The next call was tough. Helen Wallace was a bitch who needed (yesterday) a casual Hawaiian wardrobe for a weekend conference.

"I don't have time to shit," Helen shared.

Hawaii? Alaska? Peggy wasn't phased. At discount stores, the merchandise never coincided with seasons.

"Thirty-six, 5'6", 122, 34B, 9N, high-waist, flat ass, light ash brown," Helen said, "No bikini, I got stretch marks."

It was not easy to bond with Helen's cause. However, one's best work is not always fueled by inspiration. By noon, Peggy had assembled two wrap-around skirts (white duck and red check), three sleeveless Ts, a high-cut Speedo tank, a rayon fish-print sundress, black patent slides, burgundy sarong, and a short silk nightie (in case she seduced a conferee).

Helen Wallace rifled through the clothes, rejected the nightgown, paid the fee, and left without a word of thanks.

Peggy's phone rang steadily. Most of her customers were women at the end of their wits and schedules, but men called, too.

Additional observations related to shopping:

- Never trust a man to describe a woman accurately
- Men's impressions are generally vague
- Men and women never agree on what's attractive
- If men had their way, a woman would never cut her hair or wear loose pants

After six weeks, Peggy was running in the red. She would have continued to build the business if it hadn't been for Millie Stern.

"I got a date Saturday night with Mr. Right," Millie confided to Peggy. Already, that sounded wrong.

"Do you know where he's taking you, Millie?"

"I'm taking him," she roared. "I call him 'last chance.' I got two tickets for a cruise on the San Francisco Bay. They got music, champagne, they got everything. It's my birthday."

"Congratulations. Age and weight?"

"Ninety-one and ninety-one!" Millie laughed hysterically. "My grandchildren call me 'the incredible shrinking Millie.' My coloring ain't good. I can't describe it. Oatmeal, maybe. Before you see the color, you see the pores and moles. My hair ain't good either. Almost all of it come out. But I got a real human hair chestnut wig. Now, I need a dress, something with zip."

"I'm sure I can find something comfortable," Peggy said.

"Forget comfort, I'm wearing mules. They kill me, but I can dance in anything. My legs still got something going."

Peggy pictured it perfectly: size 2 – 4 (petite), milk chocolate silk or synthetic with three-quarter trumpet sleeves, hemmed at the knee, and a scoop neck. She even envisioned Millie Stern, dancing to a cruise trio that only played The Beatles. When the tempo picked up, Mr. Right wanted to sit down.

"Last dance, last chance!" Millie laughed gaily.

Like a hyena, Mr. Right thought.

At the end of the evening, the pleasure yacht chugged back to the pier. Along the Embarcadero, the Royal palms swayed in time to the music. The ship's hull tapped the dock as Millie clutched her brown pleated bodice and sank to the deck. Mr. Right was not so agile. He couldn't bend over, but he shouted effectively. It was no use. Millie Stern was dead.

Peggy called Millie back. "Maybe one of your daughters can help you," she said.

"They dress like bags," Millie complained.

"Something came up." Peggy said firmly. There was no way she was shopping for a shroud.

All week, she checked the obituaries, but Millie Stern's did not appear until the following Sunday. *The Chronicle* featured an article on the life and times of Mildred Gross Stern who died on a Bay cruise.

> Miss Gross had been a member of the Isadorables, Isadora Duncan's famous dance troupe. She settled in San Francisco during World War II and married art dealer, Stanley Stern. She is survived by two daughters, five grandchildren, and a French bulldog, Diagliev. Her original costume wardrobe will be donated to the Isadora Duncan archive.

One day, Millie's grandchildren would recall her liveliness and remember she died dancing in her nineties. "On a blind date," they would marvel.

That afternoon, Peggy removed the flyers from the telephone poles. She disconnected her number. She notified her regulars that she had lost her touch.

Malled

"Are you going to wear the right clothes?" That was my daughter on the phone with her father, discussing a back-to-school shopping excursion to a suburban mall. The question was actually an admonishment, identical to the questions exasperated women have asked him all his life. "Are you going to wear the right clothes?" Meaning, "Are you going to look presentable?" Implying, "Are you going to do what I want?"

Eavesdropping from the kitchen, I could picture them perfectly. Sarah would have a pencil line (the color of dried blood) drawn around her lips, her hair matted, her nose ring dangling defiantly, and the tattooed bracelet of stars around her wrist exposed. Her skirt would either be too short or her cargo pants too low, down to her hips so that both navel, navel ring, and boxer underwear showed. (I could have reasonably asked if she planned to look presentable.)

As for Peter, any effort he made would go a long way. He's a handsome man and from working outdoors, always tan. A stranger once asked if he recognized Peter from Princeton. The man was surprised to learn Peter never went to college. "It doesn't matter," the stranger said. "You look like you went to Princeton."

Peter was only twenty when I met him. At forty, he's still beautiful. But more than the charm of his appearance, I fell for his humor and earnestness. He's still funny and earnest, but he suffers from an acute time-management problem. His second ex-wife is in town (from Denmark) with their son and her depressed teenage brother. They're staying in Peter's small apartment, along with his live-in girlfriend. The girlfriend and ex-wife have already been at it. Both of them confiding their complaints to me.

As a result of the commotion, Sarah has been squeezed into a tiny corner of her father's attention span. Counting the little boy, teenage ex-brother-in-law, girlfriend, and ex-wife, there are too many to fit in Peter's truck.

I was home from work when they took off. Despite Sarah's dictum, Peter had not washed his truck. However, his face and hands were scrubbed. He wore a freshly laundered (un-ironed) Oxford-cloth shirt, a pair of beaten Sperry Topsiders, and Madras shorts.

"Please don't make your father buy you another pair of $100 sneakers." I said, exercising my grudge against shoe companies.

In the early evening, Sarah returned victorious. There were shopping bags of oversized jeans, tidbit skirts, cropped tops, identical to the clothes already hanging in her closet. Sarah modeled every item, gurgling with enthusiasm while I smiled with approval, wondering if the clothes mattered nearly as much as the man in her life doing exactly what she wanted.

—

Allison was flopped on the floor next to Sarah in typical attire: skimpy tops and giant jeans, their bare feet propped on the window sill to dry their toenails. Nearby was Sarah's DJ equipment: amplifiers, turntables, headphones, and dozens of old LPs. The girls were learning to scratch.

Leah lay on Sarah's bed, the collar of her blouse framing her sweet, docile face and dreads. Last month, she tried to commit suicide by gobbling all the prescription medicines in her house. Someone happened to telephone, interrupting Leah's last act. After answering, she told the caller what she had done. As a result, her stomach was pumped, her life saved.

A modeling agency was courting Allison. Although not a raving beauty, it was easy to see her potential. Allison looked good in anything.

"What about your modeling?" I asked her.

"The portfolio costs too much. Mom doesn't have the money." (After twenty-five years of data entry, her mother was laid off with a carpal tunnel disability.) "She wants to start a plant business." Allison added spitefully, "She's out of her mind."

"With your big backyard, a greenhouse makes sense," I remarked.

Allison had no interest in greenhouses. She didn't want the burden of paying her mother's bills. She wanted to be a fashion model and drive around in a new car.

"Mom lets Maggie live in our house for free. Maggie takes in laundry. Maggie uses our washing machine. She runs up our water bill and doesn't pay a cent. Mom should kick her out or make her pay."

"Maybe, she can take out a second mortgage to start the plant business."

"Mom's on drugs," Allison said bluntly. "When she raves about flowers, she's totally incoherent." The girl's smooth expression collapsed. "She already borrowed $40,000 on the house to bail Jimmy out of jail."

I had met Jimmy, the mother's boyfriend. "Doesn't he have a job?" I whispered, trying to disguise my nosiness.

"He hasn't worked since he got out. She was in jail, too." Allison turned to Sarah, "You didn't tell your mom?"

Of course, she didn't! Sarah didn't tell me anything.

"Our house was under surveillance for months, then the FBI showed up. You didn't tell your mom?" Allison repeated, "They stripped us. They put us on the floor. They stuck guns on our heads. They thought Jimmy was making meth in the basement."

They didn't find drugs. They never convicted Jimmy. But apparently, things had not improved.

"I can tell when he's on drugs," Allison said conclusively. "He's mean. He and mom fight all the time." She wanted her mother to kick out Jimmy and Maggie.

I examined Allison's porcelain face. When we first met, she was too thin. She wore too much make-up. She never looked me in the eye. I didn't like her, but eventually we grew close. She let me know whenever she read a book or got a good grade. We discussed school assignments and her various maladies. Allison's colorless skin and fainting spells suggested anemia, but the family didn't believe in doctors.

Leah curled into the pillows, consoled by the sensational stories of her friends. She never met her father, her last boyfriend abused her, and her best friend killed himself playing Russian roulette.

At sixteen, the girls appeared unfazed by the destruction around them. They ran back and forth across town, rich kids and poor, and the degree of damage was the same. In our old apartment, Sarah and I used to share a bedroom. She said, "Sleeping with my mother was 'ghetto.'" For me, it was a way to keep her safe. I couldn't keep her anymore.

—

"Sarah Breen's mother?" the police officer asked.

"You're kidding," I said. It was after midnight.

Sarah's last arrest (six months ago) was for loitering in a park past curfew. The police meted out four weeks of punishment. Saturday and Sunday, they had to scrub graffiti off walls their friends had put there in the first place. Every kid had been drinking except Sarah. They all got the same punishment, but after my reasoning with the police, they cut Sarah's days in half. (That reduced her hard feelings from two years ago when she and her friends got busted for shoplifting at Great America, and I forced her into community service).

This past summer, things improved. Communication was open again. As I defined the rules, Sarah increasingly complied. The new school year had started well. She had committed herself to good study habits and participation in family activities. The police call was a blow.

"Does your daughter know Michelle Samuels?" the officer asked. "Michelle left her parents a suicide note, promising to kill herself by four o'clock this afternoon."

Alarm was replaced by faint amusement. Michelle's family made weekly calls to the police. Her father, an orthopedic surgeon, called me, too, usually to report that our girls were consorting with gangs. Or that Sarah had been dropped at his house by a dark boy in a late model car. "Who can afford a new car except a drug dealer?" he asked me.

"Maybe their parents?" I feebly responded.

While Dr. Samuels and I acknowledged each other as the only concerned parents in our daughters' coterie of friends, I had grown weary of our alliance. Dr. Samuels tried to scare me. His tattle tales were always the same. Last week, he stormed a video store where a young Mexican worked. The boy had taken Michelle out, and the doctor threatened to have him deported. In retaliation, Michelle told her parents she was pregnant with his child and planned to kill herself.

"I'm certain the suicide note is a prank," I said to the policeman. "I saw Michelle downtown at six o'clock, two hours past deadline."

"You're sure about the time?"

"Let me call my daughter," I offered. "She'll know where Michelle is."

I punched in seven digits, waited for a beep, punched in seven more, and hung up.

"Yeah?" Sarah answered (in her what-do-you-want-now tone). She was with a crowd of friends, including Michelle, at a convenience store (no doubt, illegally purchasing beer and cigarettes).

I asked to speak to Michelle. "Can you please let your parents know you're alive? Please."

The next morning, a frantic Mrs. Samuels called me. The family had been up all night.

"Michelle promised me to let you know," I told her.

Later, I telephoned Allison's house to check on the girls.

"Sarah?" Allison shouted disingenuously.

Apparently, Sarah wasn't there.

"We last saw her on Sacramento Street about midnight," Allison said. "Does anyone know where Sarah is?"

Sarah arrived home in the late afternoon. Her clothes disheveled, her breath stinky, her hair more disorganized than usual.

I stood at the front door, my hands raised uncertainly.

"Look at yourself!" I shoved her to the mirror. "Look what you've done to yourself!"

Sarah flung my arms away and ran to her bedroom. "I hate you!" she yelled before the door slammed. "I hate you forever!"

The Barter System

The year after my father died, my family moved to Italy. For a month, we lived in a pensione by the Arno with palladium windows and ceilings painted in pastoral Tuscan scenes. At breakfast, we were served crusty rolls with curls of butter and pots of jam, and bowls of pasta and salad at midday. Everything about our life was charming and new.

We moved from the pensione into an apartment along the river a few doors from the Ponte Vecchio. Mother (with aspirations of an artist) enrolled at the Academia to study painting. My brother, Daniel, attended the city's American high school. I was left to roam around with other young foreigners whom I met in classes at the language school for *stranieri*.

There was a young German girl, Eva, a handsome Egyptian Jew, Jean-Paul, a tortured Irish novelist, Bobby, and a Canadian race-car driver (who frequently treated us to fabulous dinners at Sabatini's), and my thirty-year old French boyfriend, Michel. Michel usually resided in Majorca or the Azores, plying various tourist trades (in other words, a pretty hustler).

We were a semi-jolly group of expatriates who communicated mostly in English. We all liked to dance and smoke and sit in coffee bars. Otherwise, I visited the Uffizi on my own (sometimes everyday for weeks). I read (books were plentiful at the English bookshops and library). I incidently learned a little Italian. Our family took a couple of excursions (Venice and Capri).

In February, Eva invited us to Munich to celebrate Fasching. We were more than a half-dozen, each of us a different nationality, riding the train all night through the bright, snow-lit mountains, north into Bavaria.

In Munich, Michel and I booked a room at a cheap hotel. Eva and her boyfriend, Jean-Paul, stayed at her mother's apartment. The others lodged with friends. I never saw Germany by day. Every night, we toured the city's phantasmagoric balls, staying up until dawn, sleeping past afternoon. By the time we rose, bathed, dressed, it was dark.

Before going out, we gathered at the apartment of Eva's mother for a light dinner of bread and soup. There was nothing in her surroundings to suggest beauty or grace except the occupant herself. While Eva was thin, wan, childlike, and overwrought, her mother was dazzling, probably only sixteen years older than Eva herself.

Her mother envied our freedom, wishing she could stay out all night. However, she worked days at a winter sports shop, and as young and beautiful as she was, she was Eva's mother.

Our last night in Munich, she asked us to stay an extra hour and keep her company. When we agreed, she excused herself to change into something more comfortable. Barefoot, she returned to the living room dressed in a shiny, one-piece, form-fitting black unitard, her platinum hair piled like merengue in soft peaks on her head. She carried a tray with scotch, ice, and glasses which she put next to the stack of her LPs (Nat King Cole, Frank Sinatra, Tony Bennett). She turned off the lights and lit a few candles.

Dumbstruck, we sat on the lumpy sofa and mismatched chairs. The records turned. We didn't want to dance to that music. With Eva's prompting, Jean-Paul invited her mother onto the small rectangle of hardwood floor.

At first, he held her at an awkward distance, arm's length.

Fly me to the moon and let me play among the stars . . .

"Relax," she teased him, winking at us.

As the song played on, their bodies (Jean-Paul's and Eva's mother) moved closer until the space between them disappeared altogether.

You are all I long for, all I worship and adore . . .

They had melted into one form. The song ended, but their electric connectivity crackled through the apartment.

"Are you coming out?" we asked.

Eva looked at Jean-Paul. He said nothing. Her mother shrugged as if it weren't her problem.

"We're leaving," we said. "Are you coming?"

"I guess so," Eva mumbled, getting her purse.

Jean-Paul was not going out, that was clear. He had a headache. He was weary of large costume balls. He needed to lie down.

"Wait," Eva's mother said, running to the hall. "Take my new coat." She draped a fur-lined overcoat around the girl's shrunken shoulders. "It will keep you warm."

The Cocktail Dress

College boys were different. They were from out of town. From fast places like Miami and Long Island with the expectations of young men. They had their own cars, their own bedrooms in fraternity houses. They were older with sophisticated taste. They wore cologne and liked jazz. They liked to go out to hear jazz, especially at Paschal's La Carrousel.

Peggy and I were often asked to go to La Carrousel, an elegant black club on the south side of Atlanta where jazz legends played. On Saturday nights, we sat with our dates at small oval tables lit by soft romantic lamps. Our tables were near the bar on the upper level while most of the black patrons sat near the musicians below.

When the musicians played, everyone was quiet. Everyone listened. The only people who talked were waitresses, taking drink orders. And they whispered. Our dates ordered mixed drinks like Singapore Slings and Rusty Nails. They sipped their drinks and listened. It was extremely adult. The elegant atmosphere, the combinations of alcohol, the beautiful brown women, the music, especially the music.

We sat and listened to Horace Silver. We listened to Ramsey Lewis. We learned it was important to pay attention. When we listened to jazz, we really tried to listen, but sometimes it was hard. Sometimes, the music got beyond us.

I had a black crepe cocktail dress with a low back and flounce skirt that I wore whenever I went to La Carrousel. At La Carrousel, you had to be twenty-one to get in. Twenty-one was the legal age to go to bars and clubs in Georgia, but it didn't matter. Peggy and I both had fake ID. We had fake driver's licenses from the state. They were easy to get. We typed out the information ourselves on a blank form, and a friend pressed them with a seal. We could go anywhere.

The first time I went to La Carrousel, the hostess inspected my ID and asked if I was Eddie Breen's daughter. When she asked, I was shocked. Then, she said she knew my daddy. I was shocked again. She said I was welcome at La Carrousel anytime.

I couldn't wait to ask daddy. "Is it true?"

He said he didn't want to talk about it.

Mother overheard us. Mother ran into the room. "Are you discussing Negroes?" She made it sound like a crime.

"You should go over there with daddy," I told her.

"So I can gawk?" she cried.

Daddy's head shook desperately. There was no reasoning with my mother.

"You can go where you don't belong. You can pretend to fit in. But, I think it's disrespectful. To go where they go, isn't that disrespect?"

I never asked my father again about La Carrousel. I understood it was his secret.

La Carrousel was elegant and safe, but Peggy and I preferred The Royal Peacock, a large, dimly lit hall at the top of a narrow staircase that featured the geniuses of R&B: Jackie Wilson, Sam Cook, Jerry Butler, Ray Charles. At one end, a stage jutted into the room, surrounded on three sides by long tables. There was no dancing at The Peacock, only music and drink. The management sold set-ups and ice. Our dates brought booze (rum or Jack Daniels) in flasks.

Once inside, we sat as close as possible to the stage. We sat beside strangers. We mingled with strangers. The Peacock was always packed with strangers who were all black. For Peggy and me, this was our first experience of integration. We had no qualms or fears.

Unlike our mothers, we were glad to mingle. We were curious about mingling. We thought it was about time.

Before the music, there was always a stripper, usually plump and toffee-colored, a little older and a little tired. She performed a slow, undulating dance. Slowly, she removed her clothes. She removed them as if there was nothing to it. She made me see there was nothing to it. I never took my eyes off the stripper. I couldn't help but watch. It was the most fascinating thing I had ever seen. I tried to catch whatever expression was on her face. I tried to read whatever was in her eyes. I tried to see signs of enjoyment, but she always looked indifferent.

One Saturday night, the couple next to me got into a fight. When they first began, I didn't take it seriously. With the volume of the music, I hardly noticed. Then, they started to shout and push each other around. I leaned the other way. They pushed so hard, they rolled off their chairs and onto the floor. Once on the floor, they continued to roll around until they were underneath the table. When I looked under the table, the woman was on top of the man. The man was yelling for help because the woman was trying to strangle him. She had her hands around his neck, squeezing as hard as she could. I could plainly see she wanted to kill him.

Two bouncers maneuvered in between the tables, picked the couple off the floor (like litter), and threw them out.

The Peacock was as far from my daily experience as I ever went. I had already figured out that it was the real world, and I lived in a fantasy. I had already figured out I wanted to be where it was real.

—

A couple of months into freshman year, an attractive senior at MIT called me (sight unseen) to invite me to a dance. Informers must have told him I was a pretty girl from Georgia, suggesting someone raw and easy. During our get-acquainted phone conversation, he took it upon himself to coach me in the fundamentals of social success.

"No green," he said. "I hate green, but maybe red. Can you wear red? No prints."

Was he joking?

All week, I scurried from dorm to dorm. I found a scary green satin skirt ensemble with dyed-to-match green heels and a cape. Under the cape would go a hideous print corduroy shirt. Make-up would be heavy, stockings dark. The final touch was a dozen bangles over long black gloves that stretched from hand to elbow.

I talked my friend, Natalie, into wearing this extravaganza. Natalie was game.

A word about Natalie. Handsome and humorous, a Yankee girl with a prim exterior (her Liberty collars always pressed, her knee socks never slouched). I learned young not to be deceived by conventional demeanor. Natalie was a girl who once invited a fireman into her bedroom while her prep school burned.

"Larry Singer," the receptionist announced.

Natalie wobbled into the dormitory lobby.

"Larry?" She giggled to disguise her phony Southern drawl.

Larry Singer, dressed in a tuxedo and holding a corsage, was puzzled but polite. Here was an apparition beyond bad taste.

Meanwhile, I waited on the stairs, peeping over the bannister, preparing for my stylish entrance. The entrance was aborted. I became convulsed with laughter and wet my pants as I watched Larry Singer seize Natalie's bedizened arm and march her outside.

"Can we walk slower?" She panicked as he opened the door to his idling sports car.

When a girl attired in a sleek black cocktail dress appeared at the end of the block, Natalie pointed, "I'm not your date! I'm not your date!"

For a moment, Larry was confused and ultimately disappointed. He liked the gaudy outfit and the spunky girl with the ridiculous hair switch in the middle of her forehead.

As for me, my wits had been poured into my alter ego. In person, I was shy and reserved, intimidated by MIT upperclassman, Larry Singer. Our minute of fun was over before we began.

—

Off and on, I had boyfriends, but Natalie was ever faithful to one, her high school sweetheart who lived back in Rhode Island, troubled and wild.

"I love him," she declared ardently. I didn't doubt it, even after she divulged that he had slept with all her friends. I was the only girl in the world she trusted.

Predictably, the next year a pregnant Natalie left college, married Phillip, and moved to an apartment in Englewood, New Jersey. Whenever I passed through New York, I stopped to visit her and the baby.

The following summer, a sales conference brought Phillip to Atlanta. His first evening in town he called me. "Come meet me for dinner," he pleaded.

I didn't hesitate. After all, we were friends, too. I looked forward to recent news and photos of the baby.

I put on my black cocktail dress and joined Phillip in the bar of his downtown hotel. Dinner for him was peanuts and drink. After watching him get smashed and learning that the dining room had closed, I rose to go.

Apologetic, he walked me to the parking lot. He asked that I not mention his drinking to Natalie. As I leaned forward to give him a friendly hug, Phillip leaned, too. He groped my breast, toppled to the ground, and cut his face.

"Fuck!" he moaned and threw up.

I helped straighten him to standing. I found a tissue to press against his cut. I offered to take him to the hospital.

"Get!" he shouted furiously, yanking the spaghetti strap of my dress and ripping it from the seam. "Get out of here!"

My next letter to Natalie was cautious. Her response, distant and cool. I wrote again. No answer. I sent a birthday present to the baby. No thank-you note. I attempted contact until two years later, my Christmas card was returned with no forwarding address.

I blamed it on the dress.

Hats and Rags

Peggy finds it difficult, nearly impossible to say "no," and all its variations: *no thank you, not interested, please another time, scram.* Which made it no surprise to learn that in celebration of the millennium, she vowed to give a small contribution to anyone who asked for a handout.

Berkeley is a town filled with homeless people and any number of opportunities for Peggy to exercise her one-thousandth year resolution. On January 1, 2000, she set out, her pockets jangling with change. But no matter how many forlorn and desperate individuals she encountered, no one asked for anything.

For weeks, wherever she walked (library, grocery store, post-office), she stayed alert for beggars. She resorted to eye contact. She smiled. Still, no one asked.

In February, she made dinner plans with friends in San Francisco. It was a cold, tempestuous night, but she deliberately didn't drive. The train, she reasoned, would drop her a few unsavory blocks from the restaurant. En route, she was bound to be accosted by hapless men, camped between Market and Van Ness.

She dressed warmly in boots, a heavy winter coat, lined gloves, and a large velvet hat shaped like a Renaissance envelope. She exited the train at Civic Center station, stumbling past huddles of shivering souls wrapped in ponchos and tarps. But instead of conducting their proper business of panhandling, they were enthralled by her hat.

"Love that hat!"

"Swell hat, missus!"

"Where'd you get that hat?"

Peggy's dinner companions offered her a lift back to the train. One last time, her eyes swept the street for solicitors. The weather was stormy, the sidewalks empty, her expectations dashed. Not even an excursion into urban blight could initiate her millennium promise.

As she entered the station, a deformed bundle hobbled towards her. His runny eyes lighted on hers. Here was a potential candidate. He studied her head and raised his hands to approximate the size of her hat.

"Something got on your head?" he babbled, touching his filthy hair.

"A hat," Peggy assured him.

"You got money?"

She nearly hugged him, reaching for her wallet, but instead of heaps of change and small bills, there was only a single hundred-dollar bill, the remainder of a paycheck meant to last a week.

"I guess not," she said.

The man was not deterred. He followed Peggy on board the train. He burrowed into the seat next to her. "What about money?" he asked, addressing her hat.

She turned to a well-dressed passenger across the aisle.

"Could you possibly change a hundred?"

"That's a beautiful hat," he commented.

"Apparently," she smiled.

"Next stop, I got to go," the wretch complained.

The pink gentleman lifted a cumbersome box from his lap, unbuttoned his tweed overcoat, reached inside his breast pocket, and from a hefty wallet, counted out $89 in small bills. "How much did you intend to give him?"

"I can't let you," Peggy stuttered.

"What do you care?" the beggar argued.

"But I wanted to," she stammered.

Ignoring her objections, the stranger handed ten dollars to the homeless man who scurried away as the subway doors closed.

Nearly Naked

I was not always a good swimmer. As a child, I went to the pool and paddled around the shallow water. As a teen, I lay on a recliner on the pool deck, lathered in a tanning concoction of Mercurochrome and baby oil, playing canasta with friends. Although I learned to execute the motions of swimming, a short length exhausted me. I suspected poor lungs (hereditary) and zero endurance (smoking since thirteen).

Twenty years later, I sat in a pool-side bleacher, watching my children learn to swim. Nearby, lap swimmers plowed up and down the lanes, moving as effortlessly through water as birds do in air. I longed to join them. After I signed up for adult swimming lessons, I learned my failure to cross the pool was unrelated to pulmonary function or genes. Rather, I suffered from the habit of holding my breath. Underwater, I held my breath. When my breath expired, so did I. No wonder it felt like dying.

Swimming taught me the importance of form: maximum efficiency with as little effort as possible. To breathe, the body rolls (the head should not crane, twist, or rise). On the downstroke of the arm, the elbows lift like wings, the hand snakes through the water in an S curve, and the thumb grazes the thigh. The kicking motion originates in the pelvis, not the thighs, knees, ankles, or feet. The legs extend straight but not locked like oars. Form was exact in contrast to the messiness of everything else.

When I swam, I wore cheap suits. Cheap or not, the chemicals demolished them within months. They lost their shape, the rear-end bagged, the bodice sagged. One hundred percent nylon suits faded but never wore out. They were so indestructible, the manufacturers stopped making them.

Through my checkered career in restaurants and offices, I swam for sanity and health. I swam in all weather, foul and fair. I developed a preference for swimming in winter in outdoor (heated) pools when the storms kept most everyone else away.

A boyfriend used to say the most exercise he got was listening to me talk about swimming.

Swimming got me accustomed to seeing people naked and nearly naked, all kinds of people, usually more attractive without clothes and hard to recognize on the street when they were dressed. A certain woman fascinated me. I couldn't imagine how old she was. One day in the locker room, she passed around the gold medals she had won at a Masters competition in Japan.

"There aren't many competitors left in my category," she said.

That was my cue. "What category?"

"Eighty-five and over," she said.

While I cherished the antisocial silence of swimming, eventually I met an attractive man who swam, too. Unlike me, Roy didn't worship swimming. He wasn't transported by horizontality and buoyancy. Nevertheless, we shared the habit of swimming. Wherever we traveled, we sought out places with pools.

The Biltmore Hotel in Coral Gables is world famous for its lake-size pit, the largest free-form pool in the hemisphere. Sadly, our weekend there coincided with a rare Florida ice-storm. For two days, the temperature hovered at freezing. However, I wasn't leaving until I swam in the Biltmore's (unheated) pool. Astonished bystanders (dressed in down jackets) watched me dive in. After one breathless length, I emerged with uncontrollable shivers. Roy stood by with towels and a coat. When we reached our room, he debated whether to call a doctor. Instead, he put me in a hot bath, dosed me with pots of hot tea, and the deep chill resolved.

In Berkeley, there were many choices of pools: public (4), university (4), the fabulous tiled indoor pool in a solarium at the City Club (designed by Julia Morgan), YMCA (2), and private membership at the Claremont Hotel.

I swam in all of them, but my favorite was West Campus, an orphan public pool. Luxury and architectural detail could not compete with the marvels of this humble oasis. Credit went entirely to Yassir, lifeguard as well as imam at a Sufi mosque and master of oud. He transformed the decrepit surroundings into the Maghreb congeniality of the hammam. He played recordings of North African music. He introduced everyone by first name. He put swimmers in lanes with compatible partners. When he was absent (to visit his mother in Morocco), the place was entirely different.

"I am the servant of the pool," he explained to me. "In Islam, to be a servant is the highest calling."

After I recovered from Roy, I met a lovely man who didn't swim. He admired swimming but couldn't raise his legs to the surface of the water. He once tried to swim and almost drowned. He liked to accompany me to the pool where he sat and read.

By way of encouragement, I introduced him to Yassir. Yassir told him anyone could learn to swim. Yassir offered to teach him. He was surprised by Yassir's generosity, but I explained what it meant to be "a servant of the pool." He said I made swimming sound like a cult.

After a few months, he suggested I join a gym and start slimming my thighs. He complained about the chlorine smell on my skin and green tinge in my hair. He didn't understand how I could stand the repetition.

"Over and over," he shouted during our first fight.

"It's thrilling," I cried out passionately. To be liberated from gravity and move through water, propelled and relaxed at the same time.

When he accused me of polymorphic perversity, I confessed the disposition of my true nature. "I wish I could live naked like an animal by a river."

"Like an animal?" It was clear he couldn't imagine, and it proved too difficult to explain. He was content with the amenities of civilization: Italian leather, English wool, Egyptian cotton, Chinese silk. *Au naturel* held little allure, and strangely enough, even nude, his body felt clothed.

The Umbrella

Before we arrived in Venice, Donald and I had been driving madly around Italy. We had been driving in a Fiat no bigger than a breadbox. Donald was a tall man and easily irritated. He barely fit into the car. He was forced to fold himself at the waist and again at the neck in order to slip into the driver's seat. Once settled in, with the flimsy safety belt tucked around his waist, he fired the ignition and tore off in the little Fiat as if it were a Ferrari. It was hard to believe the car would go at all, but he drove it like a maniac, back and forth across the lanes of the autostrada. The Fiat, with Donald folded in two places, cursing and speeding as many men do, crossed the Piedmont and Po, and tumbled up and down the winding trails of Cinque Terre before we reached the outskirts of Venice.

During these mad dashes, first south, then west, then east, Donald and I were generally at odds. Questioning silently and aloud, aloud to each other or muttering alone to ourselves, what originally brought us together.

He so desperately wanted everything I was not. I couldn't blame him. He wanted someone younger. That could not be helped. Someone with less of a past. Someone to start a fresh, uncomplicated family. I understood. They were simple, human, reasonable desires.

But Donald, like most people, was deeply ambivalent. As soon as these longings for someone else rose inside him, he reversed himself. Or resigned himself. And with a desperation equally confused, he avowed, at least theoretically, that I was the only woman in the world he wanted after all.

Despite my limitations and complications, my off-spring, my stature, breast size, and mother, I met many of his qualifications. I was sufficiently pretty to please him. I dressed and cooked well enough. I spoke French. His friends approved of me. And most important of all, I put up with him.

My fondness for him was less exact. His height, his academic credentials, his stylish clothes were negligible. Typically, I adored irregular, unschooled, sloppy men. What I treasured most about Donald was his reliability. He was a test case for my own maturity. With him, I would discover whether I had the capacity to love a man who bore a shred of responsibility towards me. For that alone, I tolerated his critiques of my children, my taste in movies, and my boiled-wool coat.

Donald and I were neither married nor engaged. However, two years of companionship lay behind us. Recently, in an act of gallantry, he had moved from San Francisco to live in my hillside cottage. Despite its many charms, its proximity to the university and the rose garden, its view of the Bay, the structure was too small for a tall, temperamental man.

He was a poor sleeper. He struggled through the night. Mornings were no less daunting. He often had to tiptoe past my small son whose bed was on the landing. Or pass through my daughter's room to reach the toilet. Or sidle into the kitchen. It was not a house Donald would call commodious or charming at all.

One day unprovoked, he tossed the blender through the kitchen window. He tossed it in a fit. The heavy hillside fog jumped aside as the appliance, its chord trailing behind like a rat's tail, rolled down a bank of soggy eucalyptus leaves. At my feet were the shards of glass scattered over the kitchen floor. Not only the blender, but the peace of morning, the reverie that precariously accompanies the few minutes between waking and breakfast, had been shattered.

The children looked on in horror. The initial horror, of course, was witnessing an adult behaving like a naughty child. That swiftly passed into anxious anticipation of what a man who turned small appliances into missiles would do next.

The penance for my careless past had ended. The test case was over. I took my children's hands and looking wistfully through the broken window, I insisted he move out.

Donald departed immediately. But by day's end, he had returned with a lease on a large house and a humble promise to behave. These were the tangible first steps towards a long-term commitment, but he fretted whether they were the wrong steps. He continued to question and doubt. He hoped, we both hoped, a trip to Italy would vanquish his indecision and our mutual misgivings.

On the terra firma side of Venice, Donald parked the Fiat. From there, we carried our bags to the station and boarded a vaporetto to take us down the Grand Canal. Barges with garbage and gladioli, crates of cabbages and hardware, gondolas with brides, businessmen, and tourists floated by. The watery horizon receded into more water.

Years before, I had visited Venice. What was clear to me then was still clear. I did not like the dreaminess of a sinking city. Or its overpopulation of cats. Or the extravagance of San Marco. It was a city in love with itself. A feminine bejeweled city, spoiled by its own hand.

We found our crumbling pensione on a quiet alley that stank of piss. We dumped the bags and set out to explore. The weather was nasty. Clouds and water boiled. Sidewalks buckled like the ribs of a boat. The bilious gloom soon turned to rain.

Overhead, Donald held up one pathetic umbrella. We struggled a few blocks until I was drenched. I came to a full stop, lifted my puddle face, and snapped, "I'm leaving on the next plane unless we get another umbrella."

He thumbed through his Collins' Italian-English pocket dictionary and frantically began to chant at every passing stranger, "*Ombrello*! *ombrello*? *ombrello*!"

A kind Venetian took notice and directed us to a nearby quarter of the city. Right, then left, then right again. It wasn't far.

We entered the cozy premises. The oversized proprietress, an *ombrello* herself, welcomed us from behind the counter in several languages. We shook ourselves like dogs and began to rock in our rain-soaked shoes. The quantity of *ombrelli* around us was impressive. Stacked on shelves, rolled in corners, suspended from light fixtures, shoved in canisters, propped in windows, they were countless.

I, however, was on a strictly practical mission. Intent on the simplest solution, I pointed to a standard portable model: basic black in the customary travel style with a collapsible handle and collapsible dome that inverted like a reversible parachute and slipped into a cylindrical nylon sheath.

"*Quello,*" I said decisively.

The *signora*'s plump fingers swept the air, encompassing the marvels of Umbrelladom. Imports from China, France, America, Japan. Stripes, solids, florals, plaids. Piped, trimmed, ruffled, fringed. Some delicate and petite, others family size.

"*Perché triste?*" she inquired, plucking the sensible black umbrella from my hand.

Everything was *triste* all right, including Donald, the weather, and the Italian pensiones where every night I dreamt of other men.

"*Perché non felice invece?*" she asked flirtatiously.

Admittedly, it was the ontological question I had been asking since the trip began.

Balancing on the tips of her toes, the proprietress plucked down a polka-dot umbrella and placed it on the counter. Indeed, it was a sacrament of gaiety itself. Navy circles dotted the Kelly-green background like raindrops sprinkled over putting grass. In the hand, it balanced perfectly on a sturdy polished wooden handle. The mechanism was impeccable. I had to agree, it was ridiculously *felice.*

The *signora* goaded me with one eye and scolded my companion with the other. Insinuating that the American lady must be very unhappy to consider an undistinguished black umbrella suitable for bankers, undertakers, underwriters, brokers, travel agents, and managers. She sensed I was none of the above and challenged me to prove it.

Prove it, I did. The polka-dot umbrella was quickly mine. Donald and I left the shop, each armed against the storm. Our umbrellas bouncing lightly like two different flowers in opposing fields.

Biographical Note

Summer Brenner was raised in Georgia and migrated west, first to New Mexico and eventually to northern California where she has been a long-time resident. She has published ten books of poetry, fiction, and novels for children. Her works include the critically acclaimed noir thriller from PM Press, *I-5, A Novel of Crime, Transport, and Sex* (chosen by Los Angeles Mystery Bookstore as a Top Ten book of 2009). Gallimard's prestigious *la serie noire* published another of Brenner's crime novels which PM Press will release in 2011 by its English title, *Nearly Nowhere*. Her youth novel, *Richmond Tales, Lost Secrets of the Iron Triangle*, was selected for a 2010 Richmond Historic Preservation award and was the subject of a Special Proclamation by the Mayor of Richmond.